∞ ∞ ∞ ∞ ∞ ∞ ∞

Lola took a deep breath. She was equally confused, by her own thoughts. Von had upended her normal, *boring* but safe lifestyle. Getting as far away from him as possible was the only sensible outcome. For the life of her, she could not understand why that wasn't what she wanted.

She felt movement on the bed behind her. She didn't look back. A moment later, Von moved into a seated position beside her. She turned to look at him. He found her expression unreadable. Her pupils swam in a pool of fear and uncertainty. But fear wasn't her overriding emotion. Von didn't think so. He reached for her hands, which she was cradling in her lap. He saw that beyond her tee shirt, her legs were bare. The tee shirt was just long enough to conceal her panties while she was seated. He wondered if she was wearing panties at all.

He took one of her hands in his and leaned closer. He hesitated for only a moment, allowing her time to rebuff his advance. When she remained still, he kissed her, softly. Her fingers wrapped around his hand, squeezing slightly. He deepened the kiss, first licking and then sucking her bottom lip. She returned the affection. Von's free hand moved around her back and settled on her side. He caressed the space between her breast and love handle. His blood rushed, hot and eager.

He was embarrassed by how quickly his body responded to her. He didn't think Lola noticed. She couldn't have. Her eyes were closed as they continued kissing. But she released his hand, and her fingers made their way between his legs. She sucked air around his tongue when she felt how hard he was. Without pretense, her hand slipped beneath the waistband of his boxers so she could feel him, all of him.

∞ ∞ ∞ ∞ ∞ ∞ ∞

ONE NIGHT STAND

ONE NIGHT STAND

And the longest second date ever

KEITH THOMAS WALKER

KEITHWALKERBOOKS, INC
This is a UMS production

ONE NIGHT STAND

KEITHWALKERBOOKS

Publishing Company
KeithWalkerBooks, Inc.
P.O. Box 690
Allen, TX 75013

For information write
KeithWalkerBooks, Inc.
P.O. Box 690
Allen, TX 75013

ISBN-13 DIGIT: 978-1-7356151-5-8
ISBN-10 DIGIT: 1-7356151-5-3
Manufactured in the United States of America

Visit us at www.keiththomaswalker.com.

KEITH THOMAS WALKER

This book is dedicated to the Pride of the West Side

MORE BOOKS BY KEITH THOMAS WALKER

Fixin' Tyrone
How to Kill Your Husband
A Good Dude
Riding the Corporate Ladder
The Finley Sisters' Oath of Romance
Blow by Blow
Jewell and the Dapper Dan
Harlot
Plan C (And More KWB Shorts)
Dripping Chocolate
The Realest Ever
Jackson Memorial
Sleeping With the Strangler
Life After
Blood for Isaiah
Brick House
Brick House 2
One on One
Brick House 3
Jackson Memorial 2
Backslide
Threesome
Backslide 2
Threesome 2
Election Day
Evan's Heart
Asha and Boom Part 1
Asha and Boom Part 2
Asha and Boom Part 3
Blurred Lines
Take One of Mine Part 1
Take one of Mine Part 2

NOVELLAS

Might be Bi Part One
Harder
Primal Part One
The Realest Christmas Ever
Hotline Fling

POETRY COLLECTION

Poor Righteous Poet

FINLEY HIGH SERIES

Prom Night at Finley High
Fast Girls at Finley High
Bullies at Finley High

Visit www.keiththomaswalker.com for information about these and upcoming titles from KeithWalkerBooks

ACKNOWLEDGMENTS

Of course I would like to thank God, first and foremost, for giving me the creativity and drive to pursue my dreams and the understanding that I am nothing without Him. I would like to thank my beautiful wife and my mother for always pushing me to be the best I can be. I would like to thank Sister Dear for being the best advisor, supporter and little sister a brother could ever have.

I would also like to thank (in no particular order) Beulah Neveu, Deloris Harper, Denise Fizer, Michele Halsey Hallahan, Priscilla C. Johnson, Edwina Putney, Cathy Atchison, Lanita Irvin, Cynthia Antoinette Taylor, Jason Owens, Ramona Brown, Sharon Blount, and Uncle Steven, one love. I'd like to thank everyone who purchased and enjoyed one of my books. Everything I do has always been to please you. I know there are folks who mean the world to me that I'm failing to mention. I apologize ahead of time. Rest assured, I'm grateful for everything you've done for me!

CHAPTER ONE
THE CRAZIEST THING

"What's the craziest thing you've ever done?"

Initially, Lola frowned at the question.

Von sat across from her. His anxious smile indicated this was a real question that he wanted her to respond to.

Between them was the remnants of a meal Lola would have considered gourmet, although Von had reacted to the locale and the entrees as if this type of experience was an everyday thing for him. Lola had never dined at Del Frisco's. When they first arrived, she couldn't stop her eyes from widening as she perused the menu, which offered delicacies such as charred octopus and Japanese A5 Wagyu steak (which went for $160 for a measly six ounce cut of meat). In the end, she'd settled on pan roasted salmon. At $34, that was one of the cheapest offerings. Before ordering filet mignon, Von had commented that she should probably order *steak* from a steakhouse – "Always go with a restaurant's specialty."

But Lola did not change her order.

ONE NIGHT STAND

It had been her experience that the more men spent on a date, the more they expected your legs to spread or your mouth to open later that night. And although Von was fine – tall, dark, and handsome, short hair with a thin beard – she hadn't decided if she liked him enough to go that far on a first date, even if he did have deep pockets. Of course, that too may have been a ruse. For all she knew, he skipped a car payment to take her to this fancy steakhouse. She understood it was cynical of her to consider that, but a single girl always has to be on guard. There are no limits to the games niggas will play to get some pussy.

Back to his question.

She said, "Why you ask me that?"

He shrugged, still smiling.

Nice teeth, she noticed. Not perfect enough to make her wonder if he'd worn braces as a child, but very nice for someone who didn't have a set of veneers.

"What's wrong with the question?" he asked.

Deep voice. Not strikingly deep, but overtly masculine. His eyes, serious, even when they were playful, coupled with his voice and skin tone, gave her a warm chill, despite her reservations.

"You're not worried that the craziest thing I've ever done might be a turn-off?" she wondered.

"I guess it could be," he conceded. "depending on what it is. But if it's that bad, I guess I have a right to know early on. Wouldn't want to get too invested, if you've got a couple of people chained up in your basement."

She couldn't help but grin at that. "I don't have a basement. You know how rare it is to find a house with a basement in Texas."

"So, we can scratch prisoners in the basement off the list. That's good, 'cause it would've been a dealbreaker."

Her smile broadened. Her teeth were not as perfect as his, but she thought his eyes twinkled at her amusement.

"Is this gonna be mutual?" she asked. "I answer your question, and then you'll tell me the craziest thing you've ever done?"

"For sure. I wouldn't ask you to do something I'm not willing to do."

Her smile faltered as she searched her memory bank for something that would move them past what had up to now been a pleasant conversation. She looked down at her plate and used her fork to devour another morsel of her now-cold salmon before responding. It was still scrumptious.

"Alright," she said, meeting his eyes again. "I slashed my brother's tires when we were in high school."

Von's mouth fell open at the same rate as his eyes, which was exactly the reaction she'd expected.

He said, "Your *brother*? You slashed your own brother's tires?"

Her face flushed with heat. She nodded. "Yeah."

"I've heard of women doing that, but I don't think I've ever heard of a woman – or girl - doing it to her brother."

"Men slash tires too. Don't make it sound like it's solely a female thing. Matter of fact, I bet more men slash tires than women. It's not the easiest thing to do."

"You're right, but still..."

She didn't withhold the explanation he was waiting for.

"He was dating a girl who cheated on him," she said. "He was a senior in high school. I was a sophomore at the same school. Everybody knew his girlfriend was a ho. Her name was Akeela. I think he fell in love with her because she gave it up so easy, and before meeting her, he was pretty inexperienced. I don't know this for sure, but I think he only had sex a couple of times before hooking up with that girl. I don't know why Akeela chose him for her next fling, but she started flirting with him one day, and she was his woman within two weeks.

"Akeela had a body count that should've been embarrassing. She gave it up to six or seven boys who were still at the school and a few more who went to different schools. My brother looked past all that. He was stupid when it came to that girl. He used to tell me, '*She with me now, and none of that other stuff matters.*'

"Obviously, that's the kind of thinking a whore would love to hear, especially a whore who was trying to turn over a new leaf. But Akeela wasn't trying to change shit. She was one of those hoes who can't stop being a ho, because it's in her blood. She cheated on my brother with one of her exes, who happened to be in alternative school at the time. He lived in the same neighborhood as us. When the rumors got back to our school, my brother confronted her. She denied it. He grew a backbone and said he didn't believe her and wanted to break up. She finally copped to it, and started crying, begging him not to leave her. She said it was a big mistake, and she would never do it again. This went on for a few days. If she wasn't following him around the school, looking like a hound dog, she was blowing up his phone all night.

"One day he confided in me. He told me he was thinking about taking her back. He told me that she didn't mean to hurt him, and he knew she would never do it again. He said she loved him, and despite it all, he still loved her. I tried to talk him out of it, but I could tell he was thinking more with his dick than anything else. So one night I snuck outside and slashed all four tires on his car. The next morning, he was confused and mad as hell. He couldn't think of anyone who would do that to him. I told him to stop being stupid. There was only one person who was that mad at him, and that was Akeela. She was pissed because he left her for cheating on him."

Von chuckled, finally understanding where this story was going.

"My brother loved that girl, but he loved his car ten times more," Lola said. "Of course, Akeela denied slashing his tires more than when she first denied cheating on him, but my brother had had enough. He shut her down completely and finally made the right decision to shut her out of his life. That was the craziest thing I did that I can think of on the spur of the moment. But as crazy as it was, I did it for a good reason, so I hope you can understand why I felt like I had to do it."

She chuckled, nervously. "I can't believe I told you that. I never even told my brother."

Von couldn't hide his surprise. "Really? Why not, after all these years?"

"My brother passed away," she said matter-of-factly. "I never got a chance."

His expression was immediately solemn. "Oh. I'm sorry to hear that."

"It's okay." She sighed. "Sorry to bring it up."

"You don't have to be sorry. I asked the question."

"Yeah, but you didn't know..."

"Don't apologize. If anything, I'm the one who should be apologizing. I didn't mean to bring back any unpleasant memories."

"You thought it would be fun?"

His skin crawled.

She bailed him out by smiling. "I'm just messing with you. What I did to my brother's car was crazy, but I don't mind talking about it. It's actually a good memory. I haven't thought about it in a long time. I guess I should thank you for that."

Von wasn't foolish enough to say, *You're welcome.*

"Anyway, now it's your turn," she said. "What's the craziest thing you've ever done?"

He grinned. After a few moments, he said, "I, um, I don't think I can tell you the *craziest* thing I've ever done."

Her jaw dropped. "Oh, no, you didn't. *Cheater.*"

"No, I'm not trying to cheat you. It's just that some of the things I've done are pretty wild. I don't want you to get the wrong idea about me."

"I think I have the right idea about you," she said. "You're a re-nigga."

"I'm not – wait, what?"

"That's what you are," she said. "You reneged on our deal. I did my part, but now that it's your turn, you're trying to renege. You're a re-nigga."

He half-smiled. "I don't think you're using that word right."

"I think I'm using it exactly right," she said. "You reneged, and you're a nigga. That makes you a *re-nigga.*"

Chuckling, he said, "Okay, I see your point. Alright, I'll tell you about *one* of the craziest things I've done."

"No, you said *the* craziest thing. That was the deal."

"I'm not backing out. I'm just saying, I've done so many crazy things in my lifetime, deciding which one was the absolute craziest is kinda hard to pinpoint."

Although she maintained her smile, Lola began to wonder what she'd gotten herself into. What type of man had done so many crazy things that it was hard to determine which one was the wildest?

"I cut down my grandmother's peach tree," he said.

She frowned at that.

"I know that sounds like no big deal, but it's the context that matters," he explained. "Have you ever been to Waxahachie?"

She nodded. "Yeah. A few times. Not much going on out there. Pretty country."

"Yeah," he agreed. "Imagine how much more country it was thirty years ago, when I was eight. My mother's side of the family is from Waxahachie. During the summer, my mom would send me and my sister to spend time with our grandmother. She lived on a wannabe farm. I say *wannabe*, because there wasn't much livestock and not much land. But she did raise chickens, and she had a few goats and a couple of horses. Growing up in Overbrook Meadows, I never saw animals like that outside of my granny's house. I was fascinated at first, until I realized the goats and horses didn't really do anything but eat grass and walk around the fields. They didn't like human contact, like petting them and stuff, like you would a dog. They got to be boring after a while.

"My granny wouldn't let us ride the horses, because they weren't trained for riding. She said they'd bite you if you tried to get on them. I never saw them do that, because me and my sister were never bold enough to give the warning a try, but I later read about how horses will bite if they're aggravated, so I guess the story was true. Anyway, as much as I loved my granny, going to stay with her for the weekend or sometimes for a couple of weeks at a time was really boring. She didn't live too far from downtown, but there wasn't nothing going on there either. The only escape me and my sister had from her boring-ass house was a Phillip's gas station about two miles away. We would walk there sometimes to get penny candies, if Granny was nice enough to give us a dollar each. She didn't have a lot of money and didn't like to part with those dollars.

"More often than not," Von said, "she'd tell us we didn't need to be eating all that candy. Instead, she'd tell us to go out back; she had a peach tree that was always dropping fruit during the summer. We'd be like, 'Granny, can we have some money,' and she'd tell us to go eat some peaches instead. '*Fruit's good for you*,' she'd say. '*All that candy is gon' make your teeth fall out.*' The problem with that was the peaches on that damn tree sucked. They weren't soft and tasty like the ones we'd get from Walmart back home. Granny's tree produced hard peaches that felt like you were eating an apple. And they weren't sweet, either. They were actually kinda bitter. They were peaches by definition, but I swear you wouldn't have liked them, either. We hated those peaches, and we started to resent Granny for offering them as a substitute for candy."

Lola understood the eight-year-old version of her date's dilemma. "So you thought that if the peaches weren't an alternative, you'd get money for candy?"

"Yeah." Von nodded. "I woke up really early one morning and went to my granddad's tool shed. He had passed a few years before this incident from a heart attack. I found one of his old, rusty saws and made my way to the peach tree. The trunk was more solid than I expected. It looked like it was over a foot in width. I didn't tell my sister what I planned to do that day, so I was on my own. It was five a.m. when I started. The roosters started crowing before I got halfway through. I had blisters on my hands by then, but I kept sawing, scared I was gonna get caught in the act."

"What would've happened if she caught you?"

"I knew she would've skinned my hide. That ended up happening anyway, but I didn't think that far ahead. All I knew, at the time, was I wasn't going to eat another goddamned peach from that tree. Cutting down the tree was the only way I knew how to make sure I was never forced to. By the time the tree fell, I felt guiltier than a crackhead preacher giving communion the morning after staying up all night getting high in a motel room."

"Damn. That's one hell of an analogy."

"Sorry, I get carried away with my storytelling sometimes."

"It's okay. I liked it."

"Okay, thanks. Anyway, after I got my ass whooped, I learned a couple of hard life lessons. First, I found out that not only did Granny truly care about my nutrition while I was visiting her, but she cherished that tree because my granddad planted it about a decade before I desecrated it. She felt like the tree was a bloodline connection that allowed my granddad to provide for his descendants beyond the grave."

"Wow. That's deep."

"Yeah," Von said sheepishly. "The second thing I learned was turnips are way nastier than those hard-ass peaches. I don't know if Granny chose it as a punishment, but for the next few years, whenever we'd ask her for money to go get some candy from the gas station, nine times out of ten she'd tell us to go to her garden and bring back some turnips. She'd skin 'em and slice 'em and feed 'em to us raw, like they were supposed to be chips or something. My sister never let me live that down. As she grimaced over a mouthful of turnips, she'd remind me that we could've been eating peaches, if I wasn't such an asshole."

Despite the gravity of the story, Lola couldn't help but laugh at that.

"I don't think I truly understood what I'd done until I grew older," Von said. "My granny taught me that family is everything, and if you plan ahead and work hard, you don't have to depend on anyone for sustenance. My granny made eggs every morning. She never had to drive to town to buy them. In addition to turnips, she grew all kinds of vegetables in her garden. I still hate turnips, but to this day, every time I eat a peach, I think about my granny's tree. I think about my granddad, and how he tried to leave something for his grandkids, even though he was poor all his life."

"That's an important lesson," Lola said earnestly.

Von nodded. "So, am I still a re-nigga?"

"Is that the *craziest* thing you've ever done?"

"Maybe not," he conceded, "but the purpose of the conversation was to provide insight on the person you're on a date with — insight you may not have uncovered with the normal bullshit questions people ask on a first date."

Although he seemed like a smart guy when she met him, Lola hadn't fully accepted the depths of his intellect. She let go of some of her doubt.

"You're right," she said. "I've never told anyone I dated about what I did to my brother's car."

"And I've never told a date about my grandmother's peach tree."

The way he stared into her eyes as he spoke made her want to believe him, but she couldn't let go of all her reservations. This was, after all, their first date.

A girl must be careful.

∞ ∞ ∞ ∞ ∞ ∞ ∞

They met at the bank three days ago. Lola rarely had cause to walk into a bank, but she'd gone to WinStar the previous weekend with a couple of her girlfriends, and the house didn't send her home pissed off and empty handed. Technically, she lost five hundred on the slot machines, but she took a grand with her to the casino and checked out of her hotel room with five unspent hundred dollar bills. Considering the odds she'd faced on the addictive machines, she considered that a win.

Rather than trust an ATM to deposit the money, she went inside to hand it directly to a teller. She didn't get a good look at the man standing in line ahead of her until he turned and walked away from the counter. Lola noticed the man was attractive and smartly dressed, wearing a tan blazer with a collar shirt and khakis. But at the time, her focus was on depositing the money into her checking account and getting back to work. The excursion was eating into her thirty minute lunch break. The man smiled at her as he passed her. She smiled back politely, and then locked eyes with the teller, who called out, "I can take the next customer."

As she left the bank, Lola encountered the stranger again in the foyer. It didn't immediately occur to her that he'd been waiting on her until he smiled again and spoke to her as she headed for the exit.

"Excuse me. It looks like you're in a rush, and I don't want to take up much of your time. But if you have a moment, I wanted to meet you and maybe get your number so I can take you out some time."

Direct and confident.

And as she looked into his eyes and gave him a good once-over this time, she confirmed that he was good-looking. Lola wasn't searching for a love interest. The last guy she dated had revealed himself to be the controlling type. He'd gotten on her nerves so badly, she needed a couple of months of me-time to get him out of her system. But she stopped and entertained the stranger.

"Sorry, I am busy," she said honestly. "I have to get back to work, and I haven't had time to get anything to eat yet."

"How much time you got?" he asked. "I know a place not far from here that's got some killer hibachi."

Shaking her head she said, "Sorry, but I don't have time to go to a restaurant. I'm finna hit a drive thru and wolf it down while I drive back to work. I'll make it in time, if I get going now…"

He grinned. "I get it. You're in a hurry. I told you, I'm not trying to keep you. But the odds of me running into you again gotta be one in a million. If I don't shoot my shot, I'll regret it for the rest of the day, maybe longer. It'll only take thirty seconds to put your number in my phone."

He produced the device, accessed the phone keypad and offered it to her.

Her sigh was mildly impatient, but she took his phone.

"What's your name?" she asked as she typed her number.

"I'm Von."

She called her own number and returned his phone. "Here. My name is Lola."

His eyes brightened. "I don't think I've ever met anyone named *Lola*. That's a pretty name. It fits you; you a pretty lady."

Lola was dressed in casual business attire – a pencil skirt with a blouse she didn't consider flattering. She wore her hair in a bun that day and had no makeup, other than a little lip gloss. Her skin was fair, her lips full. She was thin, medium height. Not necessarily curvaceous, but her boobs were a little more than a handful, and most guys liked her hips and ass.

"What kind of work you do?" he asked as he accepted his phone.

"Sorry, Von, but I gotta go," she said and got moving again. "Call me later."

She looked back at him as she exited the bank. She caught him admiring her backside, before his eyes returned to hers. She chuckled inwardly as she turned away again.

∞ ∞ ∞ ∞ ∞ ∞ ∞

Over the next few days, he courted her with text messages while she worked and phone calls when she got off. He learned that she worked as a law clerk at the Tarrant County Courthouse. Von told her he worked as a diamond broker. Lola had never met anyone who could put that on their resume.

"What's a diamond broker?" she'd asked during their first nighttime phone call.

"I secure diamonds from one location to another," he explained. "Sometimes I work directly with distributors, like Zales and Helzberg. But most of the time I work with other brokers. If diamonds aren't selling in one area, I find places where they are."

Impressed, she asked, "You make a lot of money doing that?"

"My commission for moving a suitcase full of diamonds is always five figures," he said.

Lola didn't feel like he was bragging, just stating the facts.

"Sometimes I have a dozen cases worth over a million. I walk away with six figures for deals like that. Actually, that's the reason I'm in Overbrook Meadows right now. I just closed a big deal. I'm heading to California soon. I would love to take you out, before I leave town."

Upon hearing that, Lola felt a pang of uncertainty. Although she wasn't looking for a relationship, the prospect of entertaining the long-distance variety was not something she was interested in.

"So, what happens if you like me, and I like you?" she asked. "You get on a plane after our date, and that's it?"

"I'm not trying to boast or play you," he responded, "but I make enough money to hop on a plane and come back to Overbrook Meadows whenever I want. My job gives me the flexibility to do that. Or I can get you a ticket to come to wherever I am. I know how that probably sounds, if you're skeptical about anything I've told you. There's nothing I can say right now to convince you that I'm not playing you, so I won't ask you to believe me or even trust me at this point. All

I'm asking is to take you out. There's a steakhouse downtown that I've been wanting to check out. We can go tomorrow, if you want…"

"What steakhouse?"

"Del Frisco's."

Fuck it, she thought. Worst case scenario, she'll get a good meal out of it. "Okay," she said. "I'm free tomorrow."

∞ ∞ ∞ ∞ ∞ ∞ ∞

Their night at Del Frisco's exceeded all of her expectations. Von didn't merely treat her to a *good* meal. The cuisine was exceptional. Somehow, the company was even better. Towards the end of their dinner, her date surprised her with a couple of revelations. The first was that he was considering retirement.

"Really?" she asked him. "I thought you said you're only thirty-eight."

"I am. But I've been working hard, and I've saved a lot. The diamond game is getting old. I rarely negotiate with people who look like me. I make good money, but I don't like having to get over the initial reaction my contacts have when they see my black face."

"I get that," she said. "But you've made enough to retire? Don't you just find buyers for other people's diamonds."

"That's true," he confirmed. "But not all diamonds are easy to move. The sellers have to make it worth my while, especially considering how good I am at what I do. Last month I sold a 10.03 round cut diamond for $283,000. The average broker gets 1.5% from each sale, but I negotiated

10% on the front end. I haven't made enough to sit on my ass for the rest of my life, but I have enough saved to take a few years off to figure out what I want to do next."

"What do you have in mind, for your next career?"

"I have a master's in computer science," he revealed. "Software development, IT, cyber security… I don't think I'll have trouble finding work in that field."

Lola inwardly agreed. She regarded him curiously. "If you're thinking about settling down for a few years," she asked, "have you decided where that might be?"

"I've traveled a lot," he said, "but, as the saying goes, there's no place like home. Overbrook Meadows is booming, a lot of development, especially in some of the surrounding areas. My family is here. I like the people here. And I like you."

Lola blushed. With her fair skin, she didn't doubt that he noticed.

She wasn't surprised when he said, "Hey, I don't want to be presumptuous, but I feel like we've made a good connection. I've got one more day in the city before I catch my next flight. I'd love to spend more time with you."

She tried not to gush as she said, "I'd like that too."

"How about tonight?" he wondered. "I got a hotel not far from here."

Her smile remained, even as her eyes frowned at him.

He chuckled. "I been working up the nerve to ask you that for the past thirty minutes. I knew that was the response I'd get, but hey, I had to ask. I've learned to take advantage of my opportunities, because they may never come around again."

She didn't know him well, but Lola understood his thought process when it came to such things. It was the same reasoning he offered when she met him at the bank, and he asked for her number.

She knew that if she took him up on the offer, the night would probably end with a sexual encounter.

She also knew that she couldn't trust anyone she'd only known for a few days. One thing she learned from her single life was that niggas are almost always full of shit. There was a high probability that Von wasn't really a diamond broker. He may not have a master's degree or a nest egg that would allow him to chill for a few years. Worst case scenario, he might even have a wife and three kids at home. That would explain why he was luring her to a hotel room.

But the possibility of all of that being true was countered by the fact that none of it may be true. There was a chance, a very slim chance, that everything Von had told her since the day they met had been 100% accurate.

She surprised herself and him as well by softening her expression and responding, "Okay, Von. What hotel are you staying in?"

CHAPTER TWO
ABRUPT

Do not suck his dick.

Lola didn't think she'd ever had to give herself such a mandate, but tonight the decree was necessary because his dick had been freed from his britches. It was hard and hot in her hand. As they sat on the couch and their kissing turned to heavy petting, his hand had slipped between her legs, and she had reciprocated the affection. Five minutes later, her panties were wet, his fingers were slick with her juices, his dick was fully exposed, and her mouth watered as she stroked it. With her eyes mostly closed, she sucked his lips and his tongue, but she willed herself not to lower her lips to the fat head that protruded from the top of her fist.

She had already given in to too much.

Kissing on the first date was not completely taboo for her, but *tongue kissing* – that was a rarity. Von had easily overcome that hurdle as he made it past first base and breezed through second. He was now rounding third base and headed home. And although a strongly voiced **Wait, stop** could halt all progress, there was no denying that Lola wanted him as badly as he wanted her. Just as the blood raced to his manhood, making it grow longer and harder by the second, the blood rushed from her throbbing heart and seemed to head straight down to her clitoris. Von's hand was in her panties. His soft fingers stroked her wet pearl expertly, making her legs tremble and her booty squirm on the soft hotel sofa.

They had not made it to the bedroom. Had not made it past a few sips of the cocktails Von made for them when they first arrived. Lola hadn't even had time to kick her heels off before their kisses torpedoed them to this moment, before he placed a hand between her thighs, and she spread her legs for him, knowing the move would hike her skirt up higher than it already was when she took a seat next to him.

She fought the urge to suck his dick – not because the move would provide him dominance over her. Her experience had actually been quite the opposite. She enjoyed enhancing a sexual experience with her lips and tongue, and no man who had the grand fortune of experiencing her offering would deny her prowess. She always felt that she was in full control when she snatched a soul, but there was still a chance that Von was not who he appeared to be. She could imagine how his locker room banter with the boys would go tomorrow, if it turned out he was a bonafied con artist.

Yeah, I hooked up with that chick from the bank. Yup, took her to a hotel room, told her I was in town for business, and I had to head out the next day. [Laughing] *Yeah, that old line. She fell for it, though. Thought I was just gon' get some ass, but that bitch was a **whole** freak. Sucked the shit outta my dick!* [More laughter] *The whole time she was* *slobbing on me, I was thinking* **You got to be the dumbest bitch in the city**.

That thought almost made her back out of the whole encounter, but Lola knew there was a thin line between skepticism and cynicism. The spark of every successful relationship was ignited by trust.

She placed a hand on his chest and gently pushed him away.

His eyes were low, drunk with lust. His hand remained between her legs.

Her eyes left his as she scanned the modest suite. She said, "Don't you wanna move this to the bedroom?"

Nodding, he replied, "I do. Didn't want to get ahead of myself."

She looked down at his hand, the wet mess he was making between her legs. She grinned and told him, "Looks like you got a green light a few minutes ago."

His smile broadened as he rose to his feet. He reached to help her up. Lola didn't think she needed the support, but his grip on her hand was firm, and when she made it to a standing position, she realized her legs were wobbly.

∞ ∞ ∞ ∞ ∞ ∞ ∞

She went down on him, despite her best intentions.

Von had brought their drinks with him, when they left the front room. Lola sat on an ottoman and sipped from her glass as she watched him fully disrobe. She was almost done with her margarita by the time he was naked. The drink he prepared was a lot stronger than the concoctions they had at Del Frisco's, but it hadn't impaired her thinking in the short time it took Von to undress. She couldn't blame her actions on the alcohol. She couldn't blame naiveite, either.

If anything, she had to blame the dark chocolate skin he revealed to her with his casual strip tease. Von didn't have the physique of a gym rat, but it was clear that he knew his way around a treadmill and bench press. At thirty-eight, his body looked better than most men in their twenties. After tossing his underwear aside, revealing the thick meat she'd been holding onto earlier, he crossed the room and unzipped a suitcase that was lying on the floor. He rummaged through it and found a condom. He turned to face her and finally noticed the way she'd been watching him.

"What's up?" he said, smiling.

"Come here," she said.

He obliged, stopping a few feet away.

He didn't take her come hither eyes to mean he should step between her legs, so she reached for his hand. He stepped closer, until she was able to take hold of his wrist. She pulled him to her with one hand and held her drink up with the other.

"Here. Hold this."

Von fumbled with taking the glass with the same hand he was holding the condom. But by then, he was close enough, and she released his other hand. She reached for his manhood and caressed it for a few moments before leaning forward and guiding him into her mouth. She didn't have to wonder if he was shocked by the move. She kept her eyes on his and could see for herself.

She sucked him in deeper.

Von took a stuttering step to the right and damn near dropped the glass he was holding. His expression was priceless. His reaction bolstered her belief that she was the one exerting dominance over this encounter, even if she did have a dick in her mouth. And she hadn't even gotten down to business yet.

She sucked him long and slow at first. When he reached a full erection, she removed her hand, so he could watch his meat slide in and out of her mouth, unencumbered by any obstacles. She didn't close her eyes until he muttered, "*Damn*," and dropped the condom and glass he was holding. The glass still had a little alcohol inside it, but the carpet was dark-colored. The housekeeper would never notice by the time it dried.

His free hands moved tentatively to her shoulders. She moved them to the sides of her face. He took the cue and began to pump his hips with the rhythm of her lips. When he started deep-throating her, she gripped the base of his dick to avoid setting off her gag reflex. But even without shoving his manhood as far as he could go, the pleasure she provided with her hot mouth was enough to make him back away after only a few minutes. She parted her eyes and watched his dick throb, inches away from her lips. Pre cum seeped from the tip. If she knew him better, she would've lunged forward again and forced him to give it up, all of it.

But she sat patiently while his ecstasy subsided.

She slipped off her skirt and made her way to the bed. She crawled to the center on all fours. She didn't look back at him, but she knew Von was watching her every move. Before she had a chance to roll to her back, he came after her. With the condom secured, he could no longer maintain the role of nice guy. He grabbed her hips and then yanked her panties off so roughly she thought she might find a bruise on her thigh in the morning. He rubbed the head of his pipe against her wet opening, hesitating only long enough to ensure he was about to invade the right hole, and then slammed in hard, all the way, like a sailor who had been at sea for far too long.

Lola yelped with pleasure. She was so wet, there was no pain.

Von fucked her like a dog. She'd be the first to admit it.

Every stroke bombarded her clit with as much pleasure as she gave him. He slammed in so hard and fast, he was ready to blow within a couple of minutes. She felt his eruption brewing again, just as she had felt it in her mouth. She pulled away at the last second.

Made him wait.

Regained control.

He didn't resist when she maneuvered him onto his back. She climbed on top and kissed him deeply, longingly.

She didn't reach down and allow him back into her oasis until he acknowledged, with his eyes at least, that this was her show, and her pussy was king. She rode him like driftwood on a rough tide. The first time she came, she watched his eyes the whole time. The second time, ecstasy pulled her eyelids shut. In the darkness, the bright lights of their passion flickered like a flame in the wind.

When she was spent, and her breaths came in shudders, he rolled her over and was finally allowed to get his rocks off in the missionary position. As she dozed, drowsy with fulfilment, she had no regrets about the way their night had ended. The possibility remained that everything Von had told her about his life was a lie, but he couldn't brag to anyone about dominating her that evening. Her pussy had ruled the witching hour. His dick was merely a pawn. If he played his cards right, he might have the opportunity to experience her sensuality again.

Sunrise would offer the best answer to that possibility.

No matter how hard they try to hide their true selves, all wolves in sheep's clothing were exposed on the morning after.

∞ ∞ ∞ ∞ ∞ ∞ ∞

Lola's cellphone woke her at 8:30 a.m. Momentarily disoriented by the unfamiliar surroundings, she wasn't able to locate the device before it stopped ringing. She found her phone on the floor next to the bed. She stretched to retrieve it, rather than leave the warm sheets and blanket, but she suddenly felt the coolness of the hotel room just the same. Looking back, she saw that Von was awake as well. He had pulled back the covers, presumably so he could stare at her bare ass as she leaned over the bed.

She gave him a flirty grin and offered, a "Good morning," as she settled back onto the bed and pulled the covers up to her breasts.

He sat up on one elbow and leaned in to kiss the corner of her mouth, while she unlocked her phone to see who had called. It was Tiffany. She considered returning the call later, but her girlfriend might be worried about her. She'd told Tiffany about her date with a mystery man, and she didn't call her last night to let her know how things had gone. With Von lying so close to her, she opted to text her friend, rather than call.

Hey, what's up girl. Good morning.

Tiffany responded immediately. `Good morning! Bitch, what happened last night? You at home?`

`No. Not yet`, Lola typed.

`You still with him??`

Lola's body heated. `Yes. The date was nice. We decided to keep it going.`

`Ooh! You nasty! You need to call me! I wanna know everything!`

`I will. I'll call you when I leave.`

`Was the dick good?`

Lola rolled her eyes, but her smile remained. `I said I'll call you.`

`You can answer me right quick.`

Lola looked over at Von, who had sat up on his side of the bed. `Yes, it was good`, she typed. `ttyl`

`Okay. Hurry up and call me!`

Von stood and wandered into the bathroom. Now it was her turn to be treated to a full moon. He looked back and saw that she was done with her texting.

"I'm gonna take a shower," he said. "Wanna come with me?"

They were past the point of her wondering if they were taking things too fast, so she nodded. "Sure." Looking around, she added, "but I don't have anything to put on when I get out."

"I loved the outfit you had on last night, why don't you wear that again?"

"You got jokes."

Chuckling he said, "Yes, but for real, you was looking real nice. If you gotta wear the same thing twice, you can't go wrong with that skirt."

"I guess."

"You wanna get some breakfast?" he asked as he reached into the shower and turned it on.

She followed him into the bathroom. She felt exposed under the bright lights. She looked into the mirror and saw that her hair was unkempt. When she showered last night, she'd washed off the little makeup she wore for their date.

"I wouldn't mind breakfast," she said. "But I need to get home first. I look a mess. I need to change clothes and fix my hair."

He stepped to her and looked her up and down. "You look beautiful," he said earnestly – or at least she thought he was being honest. "You don't know how beautiful you are, do you?"

She wasn't shy, but it was hard to hold his gaze. "Thank you."

"The breakfast at this hotel is really good," he commented. "It's not continental. They have a sit-down restaurant. The omelets are made to order. I ate there yesterday."

"You want me to go to a restaurant looking like this, wearing the clothes I had on last night?"

"If you looked as bad as you think you do, I wouldn't have recommended it," he commented. "I wouldn't want to be seen with some weirdo."

She smiled at that.

"We can swing by your place after breakfast. If you're not busy, I'd love to spend more time with you today."

She stared at him, unblinking. Her bullshit radar was on high alert, but she didn't detect any dishonesty in his words or demeanor. She'd told herself that the morning after would reveal his true feelings for her. Here they were, and what he wanted was more of her time.

"What'd you have in mind?" she asked.

"I dunno. It's been a while since I came back to my old stomping grounds. It's Saturday, so everything is open. A movie, lunch. Maybe check out a museum or the arboretum before dinner."

Lola was stunned. Not only were they considering breakfast, but Von was already talking dinner.

No man had ever offered to spend the whole day with her, and this was after spending the night together. They'd already been in each other's presence for the past twelve hours. Apparently Von wanted more. She wondered if this was what life is like for someone who was wealthy enough to consider a super-early retirement. She thought about how beautiful the Dallas Arboretum was. Midway through March, spring was in full flair. This was the time of year when folks would hire photographers to follow them around and take pictures with the breathtaking floral displays as a backdrop.

"If you got something to do, I understand," he said.

"No," she said, shaking her head. "I have a few errands to run, but they can wait. When did you say you're leaving?"

"My flight is tomorrow."

"Then I guess I should enjoy my time with you while I have it."

He smiled warmly. She did as well.

∞ ∞ ∞ ∞ ∞ ∞ ∞

Things got a little heated in the shower, but they managed to leave the warm spray of water before another sexual escapade popped off. Von was so hard, his boxers didn't fit him right, not right away. Lola took pride in the slight discomfort she caused him. If things worked out between them, she vowed to never let him leave the house or go to bed with a hard dick that had not been satisfied.

She didn't have a brush or any products in her purse, but she did have a comb. She used it to style her medium length tousled waves before putting on the clothes she wore last night – minus the panties. Not only had they been soiled when Von decided to play with her box on the couch, but they were also stretched out of shape. A smile parted her lips as she recalled how *that* occurred.

The hotel's restaurant wasn't as extravagant as Del Frisco's, but the omelets did not disappoint. Lola liked hers cheesy with bacon, sausage, onions and jalapenos. Von thought that sounded like a perfect combination, so he ordered the same. They got a Belgian waffle on the side, which they planned to share. When the food arrived, Lola realized her eyes might have been bigger than her stomach.

"Oh, wow. There's no way I can eat all this."

"I was curious about that when you ordered," Von replied. "Judging by your waistline, I didn't think you'd get past the omelet, let alone half a waffle."

"I didn't think the omelets would be this big." The one they served her almost filled the whole plate, and it came with fried potatoes on the side.

"I guess I could've warned you," he replied.

She lifted her fork. "You trying to give me the itis."

"Nothing wrong with taking a nap after breakfast."

"Must be nice," she mused around her first bite.

"What's that?"

"To be able to take naps after breakfast, spend a whole day enjoying the city, without a care in the world. Thinking about retirement at thirty-eight."

He grinned. "That's the American dream, right?"

"I think your lifestyle is a little better than the American dream. I ain't hating though. I'm happy for you."

He nodded. "Thank you." They ate quietly for a few beats before he said, "You know, it's hard for me to take my mind off what you got going on under this table."

Frowning, she looked down at her lap. "What's that?"

"I may be wrong," he joked, "but I don't think you have any panties on."

"You know good and well I don't have any panties on. You ripped them off in a fit of rage, remember?"

His eyes brightened humorously. "*Fit of rage?* I don't remember that."

"Well, you sure as hell didn't slide them tenderly down my legs."

"That was your fault," he conceded. "You the one who got me like that."

"It was my fault?"

"Yeah. You know what you did. And then you had the nerve to crawl across the bed like that, ass all in my face. I think I should get some kudos for even bothering to take those panties off. I could've slid them to the side."

All of this sex talk was starting to get to her – in a good way. But she wasn't disappointed when he abruptly changed the subject.

"Tell me about your job," he said. "I know you're a law clerk, but what exactly do you do? Do you like it?"

"As far as the second question," she said, "I guess I like it. It's a job. To be honest, it's mostly boring work. I prepare legal briefs and reports. I do the research for the briefs and other legal documents. It's not as glamorous as being an actual lawyer, but to be honest, lawyer work is mostly boring too."

She went on for a couple of minutes before she realized she'd lost her date's interest. In fact, he wasn't even looking at her. She looked over her shoulder to see what had his attention, but there was no one behind her but random hotel guests.

"Sorry. I guess my job is so boring even talking about it is uninteresting…"

He locked eyes with her then. Gone was his quick smile and bright eyes. He met her gaze and said, "Sorry. It's not that. It – look, I'm sorry, but I gotta go."

Lola couldn't have been more surprised if he'd slapped her across the face. "Huh, what?"

"I just realized I got something important to do. I'm, I'm sorry, but I have to leave. Now."

Lola had been skeptical about a few things this man had told her, but this was the first time she was sure he was outright lying.

She asked him, "What about breakfast?"

He looked down at their plates and shook his head. Neither of them had eaten much. "I don't have time."

"You have to leave *right now*? I thought we were gonna hang out today."

"I'll call you," he promised, rising to his feet. "I promise I'll give you a call later."

He dug his wallet from his back pocket and produced a hundred dollar bill. In the brief moment his cash was exposed, she saw that all of the bills in his wallet were the same currency. He placed the money on the table, which upset her even more. He was leaving a hundred bucks for a thirty dollar breakfast? Even if she tipped overly generously, that left fifty dollars for her to pocket. Is that what her time with him was worth? She felt like a cheap hooker.

"Okay, I guess," she said, her eyes filled with pain and a rising anger.

She hoped Von would stay long enough to offer some sort of explanation for his abrupt exit, but he only said, "Okay. Sorry. I'll talk to you later."

A moment later, he was gone.

CHAPTER THREE
TRUST

I'm tired of
If the sun's shining, they lying
Credit cards always declining
Hitting up the drive-thru, unless I'm buying
What's up with these condom wrappers I'm finding?
Prolly got a whole wife and kids you hiding
Don't even care that you got me crying
Can't man up - Not even trying ass niggas

Lola was so upset, she didn't want to talk to anyone as she drove home. The breakfast she'd eaten felt like slimy rocks in her gut. But when her phone rang, and she saw her friend's name on the dash display, she hesitated only for a moment before accepting the call. She needed to vent, and Tiffany was always down for that.

"Hey," she answered.

"*Girl, why didn't you call me?* You still with that man?"

Tiffany had been her best friend since high school. Next to Lola's mother, this was the woman who knew her best.

"No, I just left his ass. Actually, he left me. I don't know what happened."

Tiffany's disposition immediately became as forlorn as Lola's. "What? What happened? I thought y'all were hitting it off."

"We were. I thought so too. Last night was amazing. And he woke up this morning talking about all this shit he wanted to do with me today. Then he just bounced. Didn't offer no explanation. One minute we were chilling. The next minute, he said he had to go, and that was it."

"That don't make sense," Tiffany said. "Start at the beginning. Tell me everything that happened."

Lola told the story, from their dinner at Del Frisco's to Von's untimely exit during breakfast. When she was done speaking, Tiffany was as confused as she was.

"Damn, girl. Was your story that boring? You know you shouldn't be talking about your job on no date. Don't nobody wanna hear that shit."

Lola knew her friend was trying to lighten the mood, but she had actually considered if that was the catalyst for Von's sudden change in demeanor.

"You think that might have been it?" she asked.

"No, girl," Tiffany said. "I was just kidding. I know this ain't no time for jokes, but–"

"It is a possibility," Lola stated. "Everything was fine with us, until I started talking about my job. Do you think I'm boring?"

"Your job is, but you ain't. If he thought you were boring, you wouldn't have made it past your dinner at Del Frisco's."

"Maybe he only put up with me last night so he could get some."

"If that was the case, there was no reason for him to wake up acting all lovey-dovey," Tiffany countered. "He could've woke up and said, '*I'll holler at you later.*' He wasn't obligated to let your date roll over into a new day."

Lola agreed with that.

"After everything you told me, I think you have to consider the possibility that he wasn't lying. Something really did come up."

"Something like what?"

"I have no idea. Did he get a phone call or a text or anything."

"Nope. I would've been more inclined to believe him if that had happened."

"I don't know," Tiffany reasoned. "I think the fact that he didn't get a call gives his story a little more weight. If it was a lie he planned to use to get away from you, wouldn't he *pretend* he got a text or something? That's what I would've done. You've done that too, as an excuse to get away from someone."

She was right. Lola had done that, sometimes in the middle of a date.

"But why couldn't he tell me what the problem was?" she wondered. "After the night we had, I think he owed me that much."

"You don't know him very well. It could've been something personal."

"Well, he could've said that. He didn't even give me time to respond before he jetted up outta there. He owed me better than that."

Lola felt like Cameron Diaz's character from *Vanilla Sky*.

I swallowed your cum! That means something! Don't you know that when you sleep with someone, your body makes a promise whether you do or not.

Granted, she didn't swallow Von's cum, but the sentiment was the same. She did have his dick in her mouth.

"I don't know what possessed you to go that far with him," Tiffany said, as if reading her mind.

"I think I was just caught up with how magical everything felt. I swear the night was starting to feel like a fairy tale. He was so handsome and smart and fine, and he took me somewhere really nice. The conversation was good, the way he treated me."

"And you was thinking about all those diamond's he's moving…"

"You know I'm not a gold-digger."

"I know, but you can't say it didn't play into how you felt about him. Nobody wants to be with a broke nigga."

"You're right. But the way I felt about him had nothing to do with the money. I wasn't even sure if I believed any of that about the diamonds. I'm still not sure. I liked him for him. I feel horrible about the way things played out."

"I know, girl. I'm sorry. I think you should give him the benefit of the doubt and wait for him to call. There's still a chance that he's everything he said he was, and he really did have an emergency. I hope this is just a little hiccup in your relationship–"

"*Relationship*? Now you getting ahead of yourself."

"In your – whatever you wanna call it. I hope this is just a speedbump that you'll get past. Wait for him to call you and see where it goes from there."

Lola had no choice but to do just that. She needed some type of resolution. If he never called her again, that would also provide an answer of sorts, albeit a heartbreaking one.

"Thank you," she told her friend, "for listening."

"Anytime. Keep your head up, Lola."

"Okay. I'll try."

∞ ∞ ∞ ∞ ∞ ∞ ∞

Two hours later, it was Lola who called Von. Sitting in his parked Tahoe, he cringed when he saw the number of the incoming call. He took a deep breath before answering.

"Hello..."

"Hi," she told him.

"Listen, I was about to call you," he said. "I'm sorry about what happened at breakfast. I can explain."

"It's alright," she said. "Can you come to my house?"

"You, huh?"

"Can you come by?" she repeated. "I'm home now. Can you come?"

Von's brow furrowed. "You want me to come to your house?"

"Yes."

"You wanna talk about what happened this morning?"

"Yeah. Sure."

"I – I don't know where you live."

"I'll text you the address."

"I'm... Sorry. I'm a little confused by this."

"You remember I told you I would only invite you to my house if I *trusted* you..."

Von remembered no such thing. And after what happened this morning, there was no way that she still trusted him. But he said, "Okay. I can come right now."

"Okay. I'll text you the address."

His head tilted slightly. "Do you have me on speaker?"

"Yes. I'm cleaning up a little."

"Okay."

"Alright. I'm sending the address now," she said. "Bye."

"Alright. I'll see you soon."

Von disconnected and continued to stare at the phone in confusion.

A moment later he received the text message with her address.

∞ ∞ ∞ ∞ ∞ ∞ ∞

Lola lived in a three bedroom flat in one of the older neighborhoods on Overbrook Meadows' south side. Von cruised by her home at 11:30 am. There was one car in the front-facing driveway. This was Lola's 4Runner. He recognized it from when she followed him to his hotel the night before. He continued driving past the home and made a few more turns, encircling and examining the neighborhood. At that hour, the area wasn't bustling with traffic or pedestrians, but there were more people out and about than he felt comfortable with.

He returned to Lola's street and made a right on the first block before her home. He pulled to a stop next to an alleyway that ran east and west, dividing the backyards of the homes on each block. He sat behind the wheel and continued to survey the area. He was not comfortable with his plan, but doing nothing at all was not an option. He killed the engine and hopped out of his SUV wearing jeans and a tee shirt. As he approached the rear of his vehicle, he pressed a button on his key fob that opened the lift gate.

Among other items in the trunk of the vehicle, he found an orange safety vest, a toolbelt, and an electric weed eater. He'd purchased the vest and the weed eater from Home Depot on the way to Lola's house. The leather toolbelt was well worn. He'd owned it for years. He didn't have to check to make sure the gadgets he needed for this particular job were well organized in the pouches. He donned the toolbelt and vest and hefted the weed eater before closing the hatch on the SUV.

He thought he looked official as he left the street and stepped into the alley, but he knew the disguise would only get him so far. In a few minutes, he would look completely out of place, if any neighbor noticed him from their backyard or bedroom window.

Von did not bother turning on the weed eater as he walked down the alleyway. Although the electric machine wouldn't make much noise, his goal was to remain completely undetected as he made his approach. In less than a minute he made it to the back of Lola's house. He studied the patio door, knowing that the kitchen exited into the backyard. The back-facing window on the left side of the house may have been the master bedroom. Von had no idea what part of the house Lola was located in, but he knew it was best to avoid the large patio door. The blinds were open, providing an excellent view of the backyard.

Von leaned his weed eater against the chain-link fence that sectioned off her property. He removed his vest and placed it on the grass next to the weed eater. He waited, watching and listening for a few moments, before taking a deep breath and girding himself for the multitude of things that could go wrong when he made his next move. He could not shake the tension that had been gnawing at him since Lola reached out to him.

Ideally, an operation like this would be executed in the dead of night. He felt completely exposed as he hopped the fence and hurried to the side of the house, running in a crouched position, as if that would make him any less conspicuous.

He felt more sure of himself when he reached a window on the side of the house that was adjacent to the back bedroom. From his knowledge of home floorplans, which was extensive, he knew this was a bathroom window. It was locked and wired for security, but Von doubted the alarm system was armed. Few people took that safety measure when they were home, unless it was time for bed.

The locking mechanisms on the window were standard. He felt as if he'd encountered this type of window and overcome the locks a thousand times during his lucrative career as a cat burglar. Without hesitation, he used a few tools from his toolbelt to gain entry through the window. He didn't think he'd made much noise, but once inside the bathroom, he stood still for a full minute, waiting to see if any footsteps would head his way.

No one came to investigate the break-in.

Lola's bathroom was modern and clean, but Von's attention was not on the décor. The bathroom door stood open. Ahead of him, most likely in the kitchen or living room, he heard voices. He recognized both of them. The female voice was Lola. It was tinged with distress but not panic. The male voice was that of a former colleague Von had known for much longer. He reached to the small of his back, where a holster secured his Glock 19. With the gun in hand, he felt completely in control of the situation for the first time since Lola called and invited him over.

Although he was confident there were only two people in the house, as he made his way to the voices, Von checked each room he passed, just in case. Turning your back on a room where a goon might be lurking was an amateurish mistake he'd only made once in his career. Before he emerged from the main hallway, he trained his gun straight ahead of him, prepared for the unknown he'd encounter around the next corner. He stepped forward and looked first towards the living room. It was empty. To his right, Lola and her guest were in the kitchen. The guest had his back to Von. Lola saw Von right away. She sat in a chair next to the kitchen table.

Initially Von wondered why she sat so stiffly, but he saw that her hands were behind her back. He realized she was bound to the chair. He cursed himself for allowing this to happen to her. She hadn't sounded distressed when she called him, but now he could see it in her eyes. She was terrified. It didn't appear that she'd been roughed up during this ordeal. For that, Von was grateful.

He also noticed that she hadn't had an opportunity to change clothes yet. Of all the things wrong with this scenario, the fact that she wanted to change clothes so badly and still had not been provided an opportunity to do so filled him with rage. He couldn't help but be reminded of the fact that the last time he was with her, she wore no panties. Did this man notice the treasure between her legs when he tied her up? Did he touch her – *there*? Jealousy was not an emotion he could afford to harbor at that moment, but he couldn't help it. That treasure belonged to him. She'd given it to Von. He doubted if he'd ever enjoy that experience again. He didn't deserve it. But if his old friend had taken advantage of her in the slightest...

He apologized with his eyes, which grew colder, darker, and fiercer by the second. He did not fault Lola for giving up his position. Not only did she stare directly at him when he emerged from the hallway, but her throat caught as relief dared to wash over her.

As her abductor turned to follow her gaze, Von told him; "Don't move, Rat. I got the drop on you. Play it cool, if you wanna make it out of this alive."

CHAPTER FOUR
PINCHE RATA

Rat continued to turn slowly in his direction.

Von lunged forward and thumped him on the side of the head with the butt of his pistol – not hard enough to knock him out, but hard enough to let Rat know he wasn't fucking around.

Lola and Rat shrieked in unison. Rat fell to the floor and rolled to his back, throwing up his arms to ward off any more incoming blows. Lola's eyes bulged. She stared at Von as if she had no idea who he was anymore. It was becoming clear that she never did.

"*I'm sorry!*" Rat squealed. "*Don't do this! Please don't do this, man!*"

"*Shut up!*" Von barked at him. To Lola, he asked, "Did he hurt you?"

"*What's happening?*" she cried.

"I'm sorry. This is my fault. I can explain." He kept his gun trained on his old friend. "I need to know if he hurt you."

"*I didn't do nothing to her!*" Rat cried. "*We was just talking!*"

"I'm alright," Lola gasped. Her expression revealed the opposite. "Please just–" She struggled against her restraints. "Untie me. *Please!*"

"*Get up!*" Von ordered Rat.

"You gon' shoot me. *Please don't shoot me!*"

"I'ma shoot you, if you don't get your ass up," Von growled.

Aside from their harried breaths, the room went quiet as Rat hesitantly rose to a standing position. At his full height, he was almost a foot shorter than Von, who towered over him at six-foot-two. Rat was Hispanic. He wore his hair short, a buzz cut that was the same length on the top and sides. Wearing jeans and a tee shirt, he was more stocky than muscular. But Von knew of his strength and took nothing for granted. Rat was dangerous, even though, at that moment, Von appeared to have the upper hand.

"Where's your gun?" he asked him.

Rat's eyes darted to the kitchen counter. Von saw a Glock similar to his about ten feet away.

"Don't even think about it," he warned.

"I'm not," Rat promised. "I won't. This is a big misunderstanding."

"Shut up. Where's your other gun?"

"What other gun?"

"Don't fuck with me. I know you got another gun."

"*I don't have another gun*. What are you–"

"Rat, if you gon' keep lying to me, we don't got nothing to talk about. I might as well finish this now."

"*No please!*"

That was Lola screaming from her seated position. Von didn't take his eyes off the wily one.

"Okay, okay," Rat stammered. "I got another one. Just a little something. It's here, under my shirt..." He made a move to reach for it.

"*Slowly*," Von said. "*Do it real slow*. Lift your shirt first, so I can see it."

Rat did as he was told. His second gun was smaller but no less deadly. Von saw that it was a revolver, which meant Rat didn't have to cock it before letting off a shot.

"Alright, keep that hand on the shirt and use your other hand to take the gun out. I swear if your fingers move anywhere near the trigger..."

"I won't," Rat said. He was sweating, but otherwise clean. He was clean-shaven, other than a handful of hairs under his nose. The hairs looked more like whiskers than a proper moustache, but that wasn't the reason everyone called him *Rat*.

After he removed the gun from the holster, Von told him to, "Put it on the floor. *Slowly*."

Rat bent and delicately placed the gun on the floor.

Von's next instruction was for him to, "Kick it towards me."

Rat did this as well.

With each breath, Lola's chest rose and fell sporadically, as she waited for this drama to play out.

Von bent and picked up the gun. He walked into the kitchen and placed it on the counter next to Rat's other gun. Finally, he felt as if he had full control of the situation. With his gun still trained on Rat, he told him, "Go untie her. Be quick about it. You bet not have another gun on you."

"I don't, man. I swear. You got the wrong idea, Von. It ain't what you think."

"The hell it ain't. Shut up and untie her."

Rat untied Lola's restraints. He continued talking as he worked. "I wasn't gon' hurt her. I wasn't gon' hurt you, either."

Von ignored him. He saw that only Lola's arms were bound, not her legs. He couldn't see what Rat had used to bind her until he got the last knot undone and dropped the cord to the floor. One end had an electric plug with two prongs. The other end of the cord had been cut from its source. Von quickly scanned the room and saw a vacuum cleaner that was out of place. This told him that Rat had not come prepared, by bringing his own rope.

When she was free, Lola rubbed her wrists as she stood and made her way to Von. Rather than stand beside him, she positioned herself behind him, out of the way of the business end of his gun. Von desperately wanted to hold her, console her, but that would have to wait.

He told Rat, "Sit down on that chair."

"Don't kill me," Rat pleaded. "I swear I didn't come here to hurt nobody."

"How'd you find me?" Von asked.

"What – I – I just came here, man. I knew you was from Overbrook Meadows, figured that's where you were probably headed."

"Oh, my God, what's going on?" Lola moaned.

"I'll explain later," Von said without looking her way. "I'ma take care of this. Don't worry."

"What do you mean, *Don't worry*? *What kind of shit you got me into*?"

"I'm sorry. I'ma make this right. I promise."

He was glad he couldn't see Lola's face at that moment. He felt her eyes burning a hole into the back of his head.

"You telling me you came to Overbrook Meadows because you know this is my home town?" he asked Rat.

"Yeah, man. That's it."

"What kind of fool you take me for? This big-ass city, and you just happened to luck up and find me?"

"*That's it, man. I swear.*"

"Saul sent you?"

"*No!*"

"Who else came? Who'd you tell?"

"*Nobody, Von. You gotta believe me, man!*"

"I don't' believe nothing you said since I walked in here. You must think I'm a fool."

"No, I don't. It's not like that."

"Nah." Von's heart hardened. "I think it's exactly like that. And if you not gon' tell me the truth, I got no use for you."

"I *am* telling the truth!"

"Fuck this shit. Get up."

"Wha, what? What's wrong?"

"*I said get up*! Head that way." He gestured with his head. "To the bathroom."

"*Von, no man.*" Rather than rise to his feet, Rat fell to his knees. "*We better than this!* You know I wouldn't never do nothing to hurt you. I didn't hurt her, either. Tell him, lady. *Tell him how I took good care of you while we waited.*"

Von thought that was absurd. Lola did too, but she reacted differently to the man's pleas.

"Wait, Von, what are you doing? Don't kill him."

"What you mean? He deserves to die. He was about to kill both of us."

"*I wasn't*," Rat cried. "*Tell him, lady! Tell him how I took care of you.* I told you I wasn't gonna hurt you. *Tell him!*"

"If you wanna do her a favor, get yo ass up and go to the bathroom," Von said. "No sense in messing up her nice kitchen. You chose your fate. None of this is her fault."

"No, man. *Don't do it!*" Rat held his arms out, his fingers blocking his face, as if they might stop a bullet.

"*No, Von, stop*," Lola pleaded. "*Don't kill him.*"

Of all people who might advocate for this man, Von did not expect to hear that from her. He had to chance a look over his shoulder to see if she was serious.

"What do you mean?" he asked. "After what he did to you..."

"He didn't hurt me," she cried.

"*I told you – I didn't hurt her!*"

"Just because he didn't doesn't mean he wasn't going to," he told Lola, his eyes back on Rat.

"He said he just wanted to talk to you," Lola reported.

"You don't bring guns and tie up people, so you can have a little chat," Von snapped. "Look, I know you don't know what's going on, but you gotta trust me on this. This man is a liar. The truth ain't in him. That's all he's ever been – a cheat, a sneak, and a thief. That's why we call him Rat. Everybody knows you can't trust this motherfucker."

"They don't," Rat cried. "*They don't call me that.*"

"Nigga, now you really pissing me off," Von snarled. "You gon' lie about yo name too?"

"Okay, they call me that, but I don't like it," Rat backtracked. "I don't like it, 'cause that's not who I am. People trust me. You trust me. All these years we been working together. You know I got your back."

"Yeah, you had my back, until the day you decided to pull this shit," Von said. "It only takes one time, Rat, one time to show your true colors."

"Please, Von, let him go," Lola said.

"*Let him go?*" Von felt like he was in the Twilight Zone. "If we let him go, he'll be back. That much you can bet on. I know I haven't been honest with you, and you have no reason to trust me. But you can bet your bottom dollar on what I'm telling you right now. This man cannot be trusted, and he will be back. He'll probably return with more people, now that he knows we're expecting him."

"No, that's not true," Rat said. "I won't. I swear. I made a mistake – I know it. But if you let me go, I promise you'll never see me or hear from me again."

"Leave him alone," Lola pleaded. "This is all your fault. *You're the one who's a liar!* I have no idea who you are." Her anger and voice rose at the same pace. "And now you bring this shit to my house. *This is my house!* You're not finna kill somebody in *my* house. Just leave. Both of you. That's the least you could do for me at this point."

Von didn't trust Rat enough to take his eyes off him, but he had to. He turned to face Lola. The tears streaming from her eyes broke his heart.

He told her, "You're right not to trust me or believe me, but I promise everything that happened last night was real. I wasn't honest about who I am, but my feelings for you are genuine. I never meant to hurt you."

She stabbed him in the heart by pursing her lips and saying, "Too late."

Von watched her eyes a second longer before returning his attention to Rat. He sneered as he told him, "Today's your lucky day. Go ahead and leave."

Still on his knees, Rat said, "For real?"

"Hurry up and go, before I change my mind." Von didn't lower his gun.

Rat stood. He took a few deep breaths and then looked towards the counter where his guns were.

"Those are mine now," Von said.

"Okay, it's cool," Rat said. He wiped the sweat from his brow. He took a step towards Von, the only route to the front door.

Von stepped aside and let him pass. He did not lower his weapon.

Before Rat made it to the living room, Von told him, "Wait. Leave your other gun too, the one in your ankle holster. I saw it when you were sitting down."

Rat stopped in his tracks. He turned back towards them. His expression was sheepish as he knelt and removed his third gun from the holster. He placed it on the floor.

Von doubted if anything he said would register at this point, but he looked at Lola and said, "You see what I'm saying about this nigga? He's a liar. That's all he's ever been."

Lola was shocked that the intruder had a third weapon, but she was undeterred. "I don't care," she said, folding her arms over her stomach. "I just want him gone. I want you to leave with him."

Rat didn't need to be told twice. He hurried to the front door, stepped through it, and closed it on his way out.

Von followed him and locked the door behind him.

"What are you doing?" Lola asked. "I don't want to be locked in here with you. You need to get out of my house. Whatever y'all got going on, I don't want no parts of it. Please, leave me alone."

Von held his weapon by his side. He shook his head. His voice was stern but understanding when he said, "I'm sorry, Lola, but I can't. The people looking for me, they only have two leads – the hotel and your house. They'll be back, and they won't play nice when they return. They'll kill you, and it'll be my fault. Just like everything you been through today is my fault. I can't change what's happened so far, but I can change what happens from now on. You need to listen to me; you'll be dead by morning if you don't come with me right now."

She sucked air between her teeth.

"I'm not as bad as you think I am," he told her. "I didn't do anything as bad as you think I did. I promise, once I explain everything to you, you'll see that I'm not a monster."

"*Tell me now!*"

"I can't. We don't have time. Rat is out there plotting and scheming as we speak. I should've took his phone, but that would've only bought us a little time. We probably only have about ten minutes before we have to shake this spot. I know you've been wanting to change clothes. If you still wanna do that, make it quick. Otherwise, just pack a bag with whatever you think you'll need for the next couple of days. Honestly, all you really need is your purse. I can buy you anything you forget to bring."

A couple of days?

Lola had heard people say their world was turned upside down by certain events. She now knew that everyone who told her that had been lying. What she was experiencing at that moment was the true definition of the idiom. She was confused, hurt, betrayed, and furious, all at the same time.

Anger was the overriding emotion, so she allowed that sentiment to sink in and guide her actions. She stared into Von's lying eyes for a second before slapping the spit out of him – literally. The blow hurt so badly, Von wondered if the moisture in the corner of his mouth was blood. He wasn't prepared for the slap and didn't have time to shy away from it. A second after she'd done it, Lola realized she just hit a man who was holding a gun. To his credit, Von only closed his eyes, took a deep breath, and shook it off.

He opened his eyes and frowned when he said, "Could you please go pack now? You're wasting time."

Her hand stinging, Lola hated herself for doing what he wanted.

But after all that had occurred, she was smart enough to accept that she had no choice.

CHAPTER FIVE
CROWN JEWELS

I'm tired of
Can't leave the house without my heat
Niggas is dying in these streets
Didn't wanna do it – it was him or me
Now I'm ducking the police
It's do or die, if we ever meet
Who are you to judge?
Too blind to see
That we're all born to lie and cheat and bleed
Can't change it now
This shit too deep ass niggas

They drove in silence for a while. Lola did not ask where he was taking her. That was just as well, because Von wasn't driving anywhere in particular. He had a plan, but no destination he could provide her.

Finally, she looked over at him and said, "Are you gonna tell me what the hell's going on?"

She didn't take long to get her things together before leaving her house, but she allowed herself a few minutes to change into a different outfit. She now wore blue tights with sneakers and a small tee. Her hair was pulled away from her face in a ponytail. She wore no makeup. Her features remained hard, marred by frustration. Despite her feelings towards him and her minimalistic attire, her attractiveness was not lost on Von.

"Start with you," she prompted. "Is anything you told me about your life true?"

He nodded slightly. "Well, yes, and no."

Her nostrils flared as she sighed.

"I do work with diamonds," he said. "But I'm not a broker. I'm a thief. A burglar. Like any profession, I started off small and worked my way up."

He was watching the road for the most part, occasionally stealing glances at her. Lola saw no deceit in his eyes.

She shook her head in disappointment. "You call that a profession?"

"It's illegal," he conceded. "I know it's wrong. But the team I work with is sophisticated. We put in a lot of work on the front end, before we ever enter a residence. For the past few years, we've only hit up homes that are valued at five million or more. Yes, we are professionals."

"The man that was in my house, *Rat*, you saying he's a professional?"

"He may not look like much, but Rat is very good at what he does. We all are. We all play our part. We were making a killing."

"Getting rich stealing from people. You proud of that?"

He shook his head. "No. I have a conscious. I felt a lot worse when I was small time. Running out of someone's house with their TV or whatever weapons or cash I could find

– that was when I was at my lowest. The people I victimized back then could barely afford to keep a roof over their head, and I was taking whatever little extravagance they'd managed to provide for themselves.

"But the people we take from nowadays have more than enough to spare. Plus they're all insured, so they don't really lose anything, except maybe a sense of security. Sometimes we make it out with a million dollars' worth of diamonds in one heist. Our last job was much more than that."

"So the part about you having enough money to retire is true," she surmised.

He nodded.

Instead of asking how much money he had, she wondered, "Why do you want to stop, if things are going so well? Seems like being a no-good thief is your calling."

Von ignored the jab. "A couple of reasons," he said. "First, anyone in this game knows you can't stay in it forever. Eventually your luck will run out. When that happens, you'll probably lose everything and spend some time behind bars. Every criminal knows to get out while the getting's good."

Lola pursed her lips. She'd never met anyone who was so comfortable with labeling themself as a criminal.

"The second reason," he continued, "goes back to what I said about having a conscious. Even though rich insurance companies are reimbursing their clients for the diamonds we steal, they raise the rates of their premiums, which hurts the little man. Plus, no monetary reimbursement can replace a piece of jewelry that's been in your family for generations. We take stuff like that all the time – family heirlooms. I know it's not right, and I don't want to do that anymore."

If Von thought he'd redeemed himself with that spiel, he was mistaken. Lola still didn't know him or trust him or even like him at that moment.

"The trouble started with our last job," Von stated. "That was the big one. An heir to the Campbell's fortune has been collecting precious metals and diamond pieces for decades."

"*Campbell*," Lola said, "you mean like the soup?"

Von nodded. "Fat cat. Born with money and didn't blow it when he turned 18 and got his trust fund. He's in his fifties now. Calls his jewelry collection *The Crown Jewels*. None of it is from British monarchs, but the sentiment is the same - how old some of the pieces are. How beautiful, rare, expensive. It took over a month to figure out a plan to get in there and make out with everything we could.

"I knew it was gonna be a nice haul, so my dumb ass announced that I was retiring after that job. At the time, I didn't think it would be a problem. I'd been working with my team for years. We all got along, as far as the work we did together. Everybody in the group has their own lives and their own things going on. Personally, I wouldn't have cared if one of them decided to walk away, but they felt differently about me. Saul did, at least."

His story was getting more convoluted, but Lola was keeping up. "Who's Saul?"

"He's the mastermind of our operation," Von told her. "The shot caller. Lives in a mansion. He brought the team together, provides the logistics and equipment we need. He never enters a property, never puts himself at risk. But we couldn't pull off any of our jobs without him. Even still, he never takes the lion's share of our earnings. Everything has always been divided evenly between the five of us.

"We expected to make out with fifteen million in diamonds from the Campbell's mansion. Most of his precious gems were set in jewelry, but he had one of the largest collections of unset diamonds in the country. That's what we were after. I told Saul I wanted to take my three mil' and call it quits. A couple of days before the job, I started to get this weird feeling. Saul usually takes a few days, sometimes up to a month to move the diamonds. I started to wonder if he would pay me if it took that long. Maybe he'd think that since I didn't work for him anymore, he might as well keep my share. Ain't no honor among thieves. I'm sure you heard that before..."

She nodded without speaking. Despite her feelings about him, she was intrigued by his story.

"So," he said, "I told Saul I wanted to take my cut right after we finished the job. I wanted to take my share of the diamonds and move them myself. Saul didn't like that idea. For one, he said it would be impossible to say how much our haul was worth until he shopped it around to his buyers. He also thought it would be too risky for me to try it on my own. If I got caught trying to sell the diamonds, he figured I'd roll on him to keep myself out of prison."

Lola thought those concerns were reasonable. She remained quiet.

"But I stood my ground, and Saul eventually backed down. He said he'd find a way to make it work. We shook on it, and we pulled off the job without a hitch. The only problem was Saul planned to double-cross me. He planned to give me fake diamonds after the job was done and send me on my way. If I came back later complaining about what he did, he'd take me out of the picture completely."

"He was gonna kill you?"

"If it came to that," Von confirmed. "But more likely, he was betting on me not coming back at all. He knows I have a nest egg, over a million and a half stashed in different banks. Instead of running back to Saul, pissed about what he did to me, he figured I'd charge it to the game and move on with my life and the money I already had."

"Is that what you would've done?" Lola wondered.

He nodded. "Probably. Saul is very well protected, and I'm just one man. I could maybe figure out a way to kill him, but that wouldn't get my money back. It wouldn't have been worth the risk."

"Okay," Lola said. She shook her head. "This is a lot."

He nodded.

She asked, "How did you find out about the double-cross?"

"Rat told me," Von stated.

Lola stared at him in bewilderment.

"I don't know if Saul told the whole crew," Von said, "but he told Rat. He needed his help to pull off the scheme. Saul knew I'd want to take the diamonds directly to him after the job. He needed to make sure someone else had control of them, at least for a minute. Knowing I wouldn't let the diamonds out of my sight, he asked Rat to come with me. Rat was supposed to pull off the old switcheroo.

"Only one member of our team was cutthroat and sneaky enough to agree to that. But Saul fucked around and confided in the wrong snake. Rat came to me before the job and offered to double-cross the double-cross. Instead of agreeing to Saul's plan and splitting the haul four ways – with me not getting anything – Rat suggested he and I take *all* the diamonds and divide them between us – screw over everyone else."

"This is fucking crazy," Lola breathed.

"Yeah," Von agreed. "But I never trusted Rat. Knowing Saul enlisted him in the plot made me trust him even less. Rat suggested I take the diamonds after the job and meet up with him away from the team, so we could do the split. I thought he was trying to get me alone, so he could kill me and keep it all for himself. I may have been wrong about that, but I decided it wasn't worth the risk. If Rat was stupid enough to trust me alone with the diamonds, *even for a moment*, that was the opportunity I needed. I could head straight for the highway and never see any of them again."

A deep chill flooded Lola's bloodstream. "You have *all* the diamonds?"

He nodded.

"*Fifteen million?*"

"At least that. Maybe more."

"Von," her heart shuddered. "They gon' kill you for that money."

He shrugged. "They gotta catch me first."

"Ain't that what they already did?"

"I don't know." He frowned. "I thought I was good until I saw Rat at the hotel this morning. I know it's stupid, but I thought I was moving on with my life. After meeting you, I hoped I was off to a fresh start. I mean that."

She shook her head, not giving him an inkling of forgiveness.

"I still gotta sell the diamonds," he said. "It's been a couple days since the heist. I thought I got away with it. There was no sign of Saul or any other member of the team. At breakfast though, I spotted Rat in the hotel lobby. That's why I bailed on you like I did. There was no way to explain all of this to you at the time. And if I told you somebody was watching us, you would've started looking around. I didn't want Rat to know that I spotted him."

That made perfect sense. It didn't change the fact that he was a liar and a con artist, but it made Lola feel a little better about the way he'd treated her.

"So, what happens now?" she asked. "I don't want to be around you, especially if there's some people trying to kill you."

"I know," he said. He looked her way. "You don't deserve any of this. But you know I can't drop you off at your house. You're the only solid lead they have on me."

Lola grudgingly accepted that. The prospect of being caught up in this madness brought tears to her eyes. "How did they even find you?" she asked.

"That's the million dollar question. Rat was lying when he said he got lucky by coming to my hometown. There are a million people in this city. Ain't nobody that damn lucky. I plan to get the truth out of him before I kill him."

Lola's eyes widened. "Kill him? What are you – how could you do that? He's gone."

Von shook his head. "No. He ain't gone, Lola. He's been on our tail for the last five minutes. You can check the side mirror, but don't turn around and try to spot him."

Stunned, Lola checked the mirror but didn't observe anything conspicuous in the traffic behind them.

"I told you you can't trust him," Von stated. "But you have to trust me, if you wanna make it out of this."

"Why would I trust you? This is all your fault."

"Because you have no choice," he replied, his eyes back on the road.

Nibbling her bottom lip, Lola asked, "Where are you going? What are you gonna do?"

Von looked over at her and then checked his rearview mirror. Rat was still on their tail, with a two car cushion between them.

"I have to kill him," he stated plainly. He waited a few beats for her to respond to that. She said nothing. "But first," he went on, "I have to figure out how he managed to track me down."

"Why can't you just try to lose him?" she asked.

Von shook his head. "Because real life is not like the movies. If I start speeding, driving erratically in broad daylight, I'll either end up crashing or get pulled over by the cops. I know you didn't have any reason to believe me when I first told you that it was either him or me, but you gotta believe me now. I told you that if I let him go, he would be back. You need to understand that he won't ever stop, until he gets what he wants."

"Why not just give him what he wants? You said you and him had a deal. He was supposed to get half of the diamonds."

"It's too late for that, especially after what he did to you. I'm sure he's been in contact with Saul and the others. I don't trust him. They want all the diamonds back, and they want me dead. Somebody's gotta die, and it ain't gonna be me. I'm not gonna apologize for doing what I have to do to save my life – and yours too."

Lola felt as if the hairs were standing on every inch of her body. Her heart squeezed uncomfortably. Accepting that she could not alter his thinking or the trajectory of the path they were on, she said. "Okay. Do you have a plan?"

"I got an idea that might work," he said. "It'll work better if Rat is alone, but I think I can still pull it off if he's not..."

∞ ∞ ∞ ∞ ∞ ∞ ∞

He continued driving for another fifteen minutes before turning off the main thoroughfare and entering a west side neighborhood that Lola had never visited.

"I own a house here," he told her. "It's being renovated. The contractor had a problem with some of the supplies, so they won't be back for a couple of weeks. When we get there, I'll pull into the driveway, and we'll walk in through the front door. Act normal. Rat doesn't know that we're on to him. One of the first things I had installed in this house is a panic room. I'll lead you to it, so you'll be safe from whatever happens once Rat shows up."

Lola thought her level of unease had peaked, but her psyche had room for more dread. "You're gonna lock me up in a room?"

"I think it's the best option. There's a shed in the back yard. I'm going there to wait on Rat. I have security cameras installed around the perimeter. Not all of them are obvious. Once I see him make entry into the house, I'll come in behind him. If everything goes well, I'll get the drop on him, like I did at your house."

"How come – why don't I go with you to wait for him in the shed?"

"Because I don't know how Rat's gonna go about this. Maybe he'll head straight for the house. But he might check the back yard and the shed first, to make sure we're not hiding in there. If he comes to the shed, we're gonna have a shootout in the backyard. I won't be able to protect you. Regardless of how this ends, I'll give you the code, so you can let yourself out of the panic room once it's all over. But I hope you won't have to use that code. If you do, that means I didn't make it. If everything goes like I want it to, I'll be the one to come and get you, once I take care of Rat."

Lola didn't doubt Von's cunning, but she didn't like his plan. There had to be another way.

"Can I ask you something?" he asked as he turned onto another residential street.

Her throat caught as she said, "Sure."

"I know killing ain't for everybody, but you were adamant that I didn't shoot Rat at your house. After what he did to you, some people would've wanted to see him get what was coming to him."

That wasn't a question, but Lola understood that he wanted a response.

"My brother," she said. "He got killed; somebody shot him."

Von nodded slightly. "I'm sorry to hear that."

"I was there when it happened," she said. "I saw it. The gunshots, they were ringing in my ears for months. The blood." Her eyes squeezed shut. When she opened them, a tear rolled down her cheek.

Von took a deep breath before asking, "Was it very long ago?"

"Yeah. It's been years. It was a few years after I slashed his tires." She chuckled humorlessly. "I told you how I never got the chance to tell him it was me who did that. I planned to, one day. I thought it would be something we would laugh about as we grew older, at Thanksgiving dinner sometimes..." She took a deep breath before adding, "Anyway, ever since that day, the sound of gunfire freaks me out. I – I guess you could say I'm still shell shocked."

Von already felt horrible for dragging her into his mess. He now felt like an even bigger heel. He wondered if he could get through this next episode without shooting Rat. He supposed he could strangle him or beat him to death. Just as quickly as he considered the alternative, he ruled against it.

"We're almost there," he told her. "It's the second house on the left. Remember, when I park, get out and follow me to the door. Don't look around. I'll lead you to the panic room when we get inside. We gotta be quick about it. I don't know how long we have before Rat comes looking."

∞ ∞ ∞ ∞ ∞ ∞ ∞

He pulled into the driveway of a two-story home that didn't fit the bill for someone with his means. Lola's opinion of the place did not change once they entered through the front door. The house had no furnishings. The renovations that were underway were extensive. Nearly half of the walls on the first floor had been gutted. The kitchen had no island, appliances or even cabinets. Boxes of tiles and other building materials were stacked in every room. The stagnant smell of sawdust and paint was nearly overwhelming.

Lola cringed at the thought of the room he planned to take her to, but once they made it there, she saw that this was the only portion of the house that was fully complete. The panic room appeared to have a normal door, but once Von opened it, there was another door behind it. This one was solid steel. On the front was a three spoke safe handle and a digital door lock. Von quickly punched four digits and turned the handle. Lola heard the mechanical lock disengage. He pulled the door open, and Lola saw the space was the size of a large walk-in closet. She didn't have time to study the interior before Von ushered her inside.

"There's a bathroom in there," he told her. "A ventilation system, a fridge, a bed. You'll be comfortable."

Inwardly, Lola scoffed at that notion. Even if he joined her inside the safe space, there was no way she could relax. But he planned to leave her there alone, waiting for either him to come and tell her Rat was dead, or she'd have to let herself out hours later and find Von's dead body somewhere inside the house.

After everything he'd done to her, it went against every fiber of her being to go along with his plan. She didn't know him. Didn't trust him. He'd brought nothing but tragedy to her life. And now this.

"The code is 8572," he said.

Lola hesitated in the doorway. Her eyes pleaded more loudly than her dissent. "Von, I don't want to go in there."

"I know you don't," he said, his expression dire. "I don't want any of this for you. But please. We don't have a choice. Even if you want nothing to do with me when this is all said and done, I promise I'll make it up to you. Somehow, I'll make it right. You have to hurry, so I can get into position."

Lola wondered where Rat was at that moment. Did he drive by the house after seeing them enter, or did he stop on the street right behind them. He could be walking up to the front door at that moment, for all they knew.

She walked into the panic room.

Before he closed the door, Von told her, "The code is 8572. I'll text it to you when I get to the shed, if I have time."

"Wait."

"I can't, Lola. I'm sorry." He closed the door and entered the code again before turning the large handle.

From inside the safe room, Lola heard the lock engage.

∞ ∞ ∞ ∞ ∞ ∞ ∞

Von hurried to the kitchen and left the house through the back door. He didn't see anyone lurking in the backyard as he made his way to a tool shed at the rear of the lawn. Once there, he locked himself inside. The toolshed was not nearly as spacious or comfortable as the panic room, but he didn't intend to be there long. The small windows provided enough afternoon sunlight for him to locate a couple items he thought he might need for the final stage of this Rat conundrum. He then accessed the home's security cameras with an app on his cellphone.

There was no movement in the front or sides of the house. The cameras at the back of the house provided pay dirt. Rat was there, dressed the same as he had been at Lola's house. If Von had emerged from the backdoor two minutes later than he had, the men would have run into each other. Rat crept towards the back windows of the house like a gremlin, unaware that Von watched his every move clearly, in living color. Rat tried two windows and gave up on them when he found them locked. He made his way to the backdoor, which was conveniently unlocked. Rat did not sense a trap. He opened the door slowly, his *fourth* gun at the ready, and entered the home.

Von stuffed his phone into his pocket and left the shed. He would've preferred to enter the house right after

Rat, but this was just as good. The Rat had a head start, but he did not realize he was being stalked by a falcon.

Inside the house, Von's confidence faded. Rat was not in the kitchen or living room. He could've been anywhere in the home. Von still felt he had the advantage, however, because Rat was focused on hunting. Von checked the rooms downstairs. Adrenaline flooded his system, dilating his pupils and perking his trigger finger for a quick response. When he had cleared all of the downstairs rooms, there was only one option left. Rather than head for the stairs to the second floor and risk the chance of encountering Rat head on, he waited at the bottom of the stairs.

He ducked around the corner of the staircase and concealed himself amongst the shadows. Rat was quiet as he descended the steps, no doubt confused about why he couldn't find the two people who he saw enter the house. Von waited until Rat made it all the way down the stairs and had his back to him before he rose to a standing position. He revealed his presence by speaking.

"Don't move, Rat. I got the drop on you, *again.*"

Rat stopped in his tracks. He said, "Don't shoot." He raised his hands without being prompted.

Von wondered where the hell he acquired all of these guns, especially out of state. He knew a retailer such as Academy would let you walk out with a pistol within an hour, if you passed the federal background check, but Rat didn't have time to stop for such a purchase.

"Please, man," Rat said, his back to him, "Don't shoot me. I'm sorry, but you know I had to come."

"Crouch down, and put the gun on the floor," Von ordered. He was no more than six feet away. At that range, the exit wound of his Glock would end his opponent with a shot to the midsection.

Rat bent and placed the gun on the floor. "Can I look at you?" he asked. "Can we talk?"

"Yeah," Von said. "Turn around. Keep your hands up."

Rat faced him, defeat in his eyes. Von shook his head in disappointment. Sweat glistened on Rat's brown face.

"Before you say a word," Von said, "I need you to understand that I will kill you the moment you tell me a lie. I gave you a chance. You said I wouldn't see you again, but you came back for me. As far as I'm concerned, that means you want to die."

"*I don't*," Rat cried. "Von, please. Don't do me like this. I came because I had to. I need my cut. Saul exed me out. He thinks I had something to do with you running off."

That sounded like the truth, but Von didn't believe him. He was, after all, talking to a human-sized rat.

"You sold me out," he said. "Tell the truth. We had a deal. You said you wanted to meet me after the job and split the diamonds fifty-fifty. But you told Saul about our plan, didn't you?"

"Von, please don't do this."

Rat was trembling. Von could smell his panic, even from a distance. It was disgusting.

"I thought we had a deal," Von repeated.

"*But you didn't meet me*," Rat cried, literally. Tears now mingled with the sweat on his cheeks. "I went to the meet point, but you weren't there. You left without me. You took everything."

"I took it because I knew you sold me out, Rat. It's time to tell the truth." He moved the barrel of the gun from

Rat's chest to his face. "You told Saul about our plan. Tell the truth, or I'ma blow your brains out *right fucking now!*"

"*Okay, okay!*"

Rat's hands flung forward, attempting to block a bullet again. Von understood this was a natural survival instinct, rather than pure ignorance on the part of the prey.

"*I told him!*" Rat squealed.

Von didn't not take time to process the betrayal before asking, "Why? You sold me out. We could've been up over seven million apiece. Why would you do that?"

"Because he would've found us," Rat blubbered. Snot began to dribble from his nostrils. He was a mess.

"How?" Von asked. His heart thundered, but his voice was as sure as rain.

"He would've found us," Rat repeated. "I know he would."

This was a lie. Von knew it, and he knew it would not be easy to extract the truth.

"How did you find me?" Von asked, a roundabout question to the one he still hadn't received an answer to.

Rat's eyes widened. He lowered his hands, just a little, enough for Von to notice his tell. Rat's eyes narrowed, just a tad bit, before he told another lie: "I told you. I knew you were from—"

So caught up in what he was about to say, Rat didn't notice that Von had used his free hand to remove a taser from his pocket. Von shut him up with 1200 volts of unexpected electricity. Rat immediately fell to the floor. He rolled and squirmed and cried out for nearly a minute. By the time his cries subsided, and Von was sure he had his full attention, he reached to the small of his back and produced a plastic ketchup bottle. He squirted the contents on the man on the floor. Rat did not have to question whether Von was squirting condiments on him. He'd come to his senses by then and could smell the gasoline.

Von reached into his pocket and produced a Zippo lighter. It was an older model, the kind that retained its flame after ignition. He lit it up and held it forward. The implication was obvious, but he made it clearer.

"Either tell me how you found me or burn to death – right here and now. You prolly think you gon' die either way. And that may be true. But there are levels to death. If you wanna know what it's like to feel your flesh burn, lie to me one more time. *How did you find me?*" he growled.

"*Von, please don't do this!*"

Rat's eyes burned from the gasoline. He squeezed them shut and wiped at them roughly. This inhibited his view of the grim reaper. But he could hear him clearly.

"Last chance."

"*It's a tracker in the fucking bag!*" Rat spat. "*I put it in there. We knew you'd try to take off with the diamonds. We knew where you were headed, and we know where they are. Don't kill me, Von! You can't win. Even if you kill me, you can't win!*"

Von didn't mean to break his promise, but the fire from the two bullets he put in the downed body ignited the gasoline. It wasn't a big fire. He was able to put it out with just his foot, stomping the corpse. But still. In addition to dying from his bullet wounds, Rat probably felt what it was like to feel his flesh burn.

Von sighed angrily when it was all over. He wanted to prepare the body for disposal and clean up a little before he returned to the panic room, but he didn't. Even with the steel door, Lola's safe space was not soundproof. He knew she'd heard the muffled argument and the gunshots. She wouldn't know who had emerged victorious until she saw that Von was the last man standing.

He left the body and headed for the panic room, knowing she'd hate him even more once she saw what he had done.

CHAPTER SIX
DEAD WEIGHT

Used to be my homey
Used to be my ace
Used to be the one who was always down to ride
Catch a case?
Never that
Get what we came for
Then we slide
Getaway filled with diamonds and smiles
Break it all down fifty-fifty
Now we fly
Now you gon' try
To take what's mine?
What the fuck?
This how money do us?
You siding with the opps now
So it's screw us?
Better come hard or not at all
The sweetest sentiments sometimes sour
Greed has led to a billion downfalls
I pray to God it don't lead to ours

Lola cowered when the door of the panic room swung open. She was flooded with relief when she saw that it was Von who had come for her and not the Mexican. She was baffled by her own emotions. This man had brought her nothing but grief since he walked out on her at breakfast. Under no circumstance should she find herself happy to see him, yet here they were.

Von thought her features appeared gaunt as she said, "I – I heard gunshots. Is it over? Did you do it?"

He nodded somberly. "Yeah. I'm sorry to put you through this." He felt like he was stuck in a perpetual loop of apologies to this woman. But they were all warranted, and he meant every one.

"I have to take care of the body," he told her. "You should stay here. It shouldn't take very long."

"*You're leaving?* I don't wanna stay in here. I wanna go home." Her words were smothered in exhaustion and tension.

"I want that for you too," he said. "But you know I can't take you home now. Rat told me something that actually makes things worse. I'll explain later. For now, I have to get his body out of this house. I gotta find somewhere to dump him, and then I will come back for you."

"I don't want to stay here while you do that," she protested. "What if more people come looking for you? I don't want to be here alone. I have to go with you."

Von took note of how she felt she *had* to go, rather than wanted to. Considering the condition he'd left Rat in, he told her, "Okay, you can come with me. But give me a few minutes to get his body in the car. Trust me, you don't wanna see this."

Lola shook her head, but she retreated back into the panic room. Before taking a seat on the bed, her nose cringed as she asked, "What's that smell?"

He told her, "Rat got hisself set on fire. Nothing big. I put it out."

The nonchalant way in which he delivered that news horrified her. This time, she was relieved when he walked away and left her alone. She didn't want to be anywhere near him.

∞ ∞ ∞ ∞ ∞ ∞ ∞

Von found heavy duty trash bags and a few cleaning supplies in the gutted house. Removing all traces of the dead man was a tremendous undertaking, but he didn't have to do that now. His contractors weren't expected back for a couple of weeks. And Lola had spooked him with the thought of his other former associates knowing about this location. He donned a pair of gloves before checking Rat's pockets for any form of identification. He then found a large drop cloth the painters had left behind. He spread it on the floor next to the body and rolled Rat onto it.

He used bleach wipes to clean the gun he'd used to kill the man and placed it on the body. This was one of the guns Rat had left behind at Lola's house. Von had no idea where Rat had acquired the weapon, but the police would only be able to trace it back to the dead man.

He washed up and left the house through the front door. The afternoon sun was bright, almost blindingly so. He did not feel good about disposing of a body in broad daylight, but the prospect of leaving the corpse in a home he'd purchased under his name was even less appealing. He hadn't pulled into the garage when they arrived, because he wanted to make sure Rat knew exactly where to find them. But now, the garage was useful. Von pulled out of the driveway and then backed the Tahoe into the garage.

He returned to the house, where Rat's body was halfway in the kitchen; his other half stretched into the hallway. Von thought he'd done a good job wrapping him up, but when he began to drag the body towards the garage door, a trail of dark blood followed him. He grimaced, both at the weight of the dead man and all the DNA he'd have to contend with. Thankfully, the Tahoe wasn't in his name. He'd purchased it with cash from a car thief who also threw in stolen plates. The plates wouldn't hold up to scrutiny if Von was ever pulled over, but if things went well, he would only be behind the wheel of the SUV for a couple more hours.

Hefting Rat's body into the trunk of the car began to feel like mission impossible. Rat didn't look like he weighed very much, but Von found a new appreciation for the term *dead weight*. After a failed third attempt, he had half a notion to ask Lola for help. Instead, he altered his strategy. He dragged Rat's upper half into the trunk and made sure it wasn't going to slide out before he folded the legs in behind him. He was winded and bloody when it was all said and done.

He reentered the house and cleaned up the blood trail as best he could. He avoided the panic room on the way to a shower. Even though Lola knew what he'd been up to, he didn't want her to see him like this. He didn't have any clothes in the house, so he had to put on the same jeans. He thought he might have an extra tee shirt in his truck. He stopped by the panic room to check on Lola when he left the shower. She was still seated on the bed, perusing her cellphone. She looked up at his topless physique. As fine as he was, the only thing she saw as she stared at him was a murderer. A liar, thief and killer who had somehow become her savior.

"You finished?" she asked him.

He nodded. "Yeah. Let me get dressed, and we can head out."

"What are you gonna do with the body?"

"I know a few out of the way places. Should be able to dump him without anyone seeing us." Noticing her expression, he added, "Not that I do this kind of thing all the time."

"You never killed anyone before?"

She expected him to lie, but Von maintained eye contact as he nodded.

"Yeah. I have."

"More than once?"

Again, she saw no shame in his eyes when he said, "Yes. But–"

"I don't need you to explain it to me." She lowered her face into her hand and rubbed the stress point between her eyebrows. "Just let me know when you're ready to go."

∞ ∞ ∞ ∞ ∞ ∞ ∞

They didn't speak much as Von drove them outside of the city limits, to a suburb named Forest Hill. Even with all four windows down, the stench of the body in the trunk was palpable. Rat had not begun to decompose, rather it was the scent of gasoline and seared flesh that singed their nostrils. When they reached Forest Hill, Von left the main road and drove towards a wooded area that was unpopulated and

83

overgrown with shrubbery. The street became a dirt road and then a trail and then nothing at all. Von continued driving. Through the open windows, Lola heard a few birds chirping and thick tree branches snapping beneath the weight of the vehicle. They came upon a large duck pond. Von put the SUV in park and surveyed the area.

After a few moments, he told her, "My dad used to take me fishing out here. We'd catch some nice-size catfish, take 'em home and fry 'em up."

As she took in the scene, Lola was reminded of his plan to take her to the Dallas Arboretum and Botanical Gardens that day. This place was a far cry from the beauty they would've encountered there. She almost commented on the disparity, but despite how she felt about him, she understood that Von was trying to get her out of the trouble he brought to her life. Her complaints, on the other hand, weren't helpful at all.

He left the car and tried his best to get the body into the water, but it was no use. Rat was too damn heavy. And the closer he dragged the corpse to the pond, the muddier the terrain became. If he persisted, he'd end up with muck all the way up to his knees, so he left the body in the high grass at the edge of the pond. He returned to the SUV, sweating again.

"Okay," he panted. "That's done. Let's get the hell up outta here."

Lola wanted nothing more. "Where we going?"

"Get us a hotel," he said and got the truck rolling. "I gotta leave you there for a little bit to take care of a few things."

Lola was not opposed to being left in a nice, clean hotel room. She asked him, "What do you have to do?"

"Get rid of this car for one. And then I have to check on the diamonds."

Her eyes narrowed. "You don't have them with you?"

He shook his head. "I thought I stashed them somewhere safe, but I don't feel so good about that anymore." Before she could ask more follow-up questions, he told her, "I promise, I'll explain everything. Can you call and book us a room somewhere in Overbrook Meadows?"

"Anywhere?"

"Long as they got a shower and a restaurant, I'm good."

∞ ∞ ∞ ∞ ∞ ∞ ∞

Lola found an Embassy Suites downtown that had all the amenities they both wanted. When making the reservation, she did not ask Von about his preference for the number of bedrooms. She had no plans to sleep in the same room with this man again – ever. But she did ask about the length of their stay. He told her to book the room for a week.

She put the operator on mute and said, "*A week?* You think it'll take that long to be done with this? I have to get back to work on Monday."

"No," he replied. "I'm hoping to be done this weekend. But I'll need a place to stay afterwards. I'll keep the room after you leave."

Thirty minutes later, they checked into the hotel with no problem. When they made it to their room, Lola felt comfortable for the first time, since Von's speedy exit during breakfast that morning. She only had one bag. She dropped it off in her room before returning to the front room to speak

85

to her benefactor. Von hadn't bothered to take a seat while he waited for her.

He asked her, "You good?"

"Yeah," she said. "This is nice."

"You should get something for lunch," he suggested. "You hungry?"

By then, it was after three. She hadn't thought about eating until he mentioned it. Now, she suddenly felt ravenous.

"Yeah. It's okay if I order room service?"

He nodded. "That's why we're here. At least you have some clothes to change into. I wanna take a shower so bad, but all my stuff is at the other hotel. That's where the diamonds are too."

That surprised her. "You left them there?"

"I had to. Once I spotted Rat, I left, so I could get in position to follow him whenever he left the hotel. I waited for so long, I started to worry about you. I felt that with me missing, his next best move was to go after you. I saw you leave the hotel, about ten minutes after I did, but I didn't see Rat on your tail. I didn't know what to do at that point. I wanted to go back to the room to get the diamonds, but I didn't want to risk running into him again."

"You think it's safe to go back there now?"

He shrugged. "I don't know about *safe*, but I gotta go get them. The problem is Rat told me he slipped a GPS tracker in the case the diamonds are in. I knew I couldn't trust him. Turns out, he never trusted me either. That was a smart move on his part. I never suspected a thing."

"And that's how he found you." Everything was starting to make sense now.

"Yeah. But even with him out of the picture, it's risky to go get those diamonds. I told you a little about my crew. I think Rat has been in communication with Saul. If so, Saul knows where the diamonds are. With our last job, me and Rat worked with two other people – Katrina and Jugg. For all I know, they're all coming for those diamonds too. They could be at the hotel already, waiting for me to show up. I won't know until I get there."

Once again, Lola felt an emotion for Von that shouldn't be there.

Dread.

Why should she care what happened to this man? If he hadn't double-crossed his crew, he wouldn't have to worry about them gunning for him. But she couldn't stop herself from caring about his wellbeing. On a deeper level, she understood that this meant she cared about him *overall*. She didn't allow herself time to contemplate why that may be the case.

She told him, "I don't think you should go. You said you have over a million dollars saved. That's more than most people make in twenty years. You could sit on that money until you get started on the new career you were talking about. You said you had a degree in computer science. Or was that a lie too?"

"No. That's the truth. Look, I understand why you think it's easy to let go, but I just killed a man. If I don't get those diamonds, then I did that for nothing. That's not something I can accept."

"Or maybe you're being greedy."

"When it came to our jobs," he said, "all of us have unique skills. That's why we worked so well together. Jugg was the muscle, in case some unexpected violence popped off. Katrina is the safecracker. She's amazing with that shit. Rat was on top of surveillance and counterintelligence. He and I worked closest together. Saul added me to the team because of my burglary skills. There's not a locked door or security system that I can't get through."

"And all of that means what?" Lola asked.

"It means the remaining two members of our crew aren't skilled enough to break into a hotel room *and* bypass the security cameras. That's *my* job. If anything, they're waiting on me to go for the diamonds. But they don't know that I know they might be there, so I have the advantage. Plus, I gotta get rid of that Tahoe. I can't leave it in the parking lot after what we just did with it."

She knew she couldn't stop him, so she subdued her distress and asked, "What if you don't come back?"

"If I don't make it back, that means they got me."

Lola had deduced that on her own. She'd hoped he'd offer something more insightful.

"If I'm not back by nightfall, you can go home," he added. "They'll have no use for you, if they get what they want from me."

She took a deep breath and blew it slowly from her nostrils.

"Alright," he said, "I gotta go."

He headed for the door. Despite how much she hated him, her compassionate side offered a few parting words.

"Please, be careful."

"I will," he said, and then he was gone.

∞ ∞ ∞ ∞ ∞ ∞ ∞

Von arrived at the DoubleTree Hotel and found a parking spot near the entrance. He hadn't seen any familiar faces inside any of the cars in the parking lot and dismissed the notion that he should survey the scene a while longer. If Katrina, Jugg or any of Saul's henchmen were there waiting on him, odds were they would spot Von before he spotted them. As imprudent as it sounded, he figured his best bet was to walk into the hotel, head straight to his room, grab his belongings, and flee the scene.

But that didn't mean he'd be unprepared for an ambush. He concealed his Glock 19 in the small of his back before exiting the SUV. He felt like he was walking on pins and needles, but he forced himself to appear inconspicuous as he entered the hotel lobby. This was no easy task, considering he thought he smelled like a combination of gasoline and burnt barbecue, and his shoes were caked with dried mud from the pond.

He breathed a sigh of relief when he entered the elevator alone. Moments later, he emerged on the fifth floor. There was no one in the hallway waiting for him to use his keycard to access room 533. As he walked, Von wondered if his pursuers had booked one of the adjacent rooms. For all he knew, they had already set up a stakeout. They might be looking through their peep hole, knowing he would show his face at some point. Von frowned at himself, thinking his paranoia was getting the best of him. Would anyone stare through a peephole for *hours*? He could think of fifteen million reasons why they might do just that.

He reached his room and held the card in front of the reader. The light turned green as the lock disengaged. Von slipped inside and quickly closed the door behind him. His heart thundered as he secured the deadbolt and the latch. He removed his gun from the holster and readied it as he cleared the small space. With only one bedroom that didn't have a door separating it from the front room, there wasn't much to clear. But Von was diligent. He didn't let his guard down until he was certain there was no one lurking in the bathroom or even the small closet.

He checked his watch. It was 3:52. He planned to be out of there in less than three minutes. He placed his gun on the bed and returned to the front room. He knelt in front of the dresser under the TV and pulled out the bottom drawer. He half expected to find it empty, but a few of his clothes were there, just as he'd left them. He tossed the clothes aside, again thinking there would be nothing else in the drawer, but the two medium-size cases were still there. They were black, leatherbound. His fingers trembled as he removed them and took them to the bedroom.

He opened the cases on the bed. His blood raced so hard, he was starting to feel lightheaded. Inside each case were 24 smaller boxes, a dozen mounted on each side, 48 in all. Each of these boxes was metal with a glass front. Behind all of the glass displays was a diamond. They ranged in sizes, shapes and colors.

Von's mouth was dry as he muttered, "My God."

They were beautiful. Perfect, twinkling, precious natural crystals. Seconds ticked by. Von didn't realize he'd become mesmerized until his phone vibrated in his pocket. He checked his watch before he reached for it. He'd received a text from Lola.

She asked, `Is everything okay?`

Von could not spare the time it would take to respond to her. He didn't see any foreign items inside the first case, but he spotted the GPS Tracker in the second one. It was tucked under one of the metal boxes. It was round, not very large, about the size of a fifty-cent piece.

Sonofabitch.

He snagged the tracker and slipped it in his front pocket. He then closed the cases and grabbed his suitcase from the floor. He nestled the cases amongst his clothes and quickly looked around the suite, to see if there was anything else he needed to take with him. Compared to what he already had in the suitcase, nothing was that important, not even his toiletries that were on the vanity top in the bathroom. He returned to the bed, zipped his suitcase closed, and grabbed his gun. So anxious to get out of there, he almost walked out of the suite with the gun in hand. He stuffed it in his holster at the last minute.

Von didn't think he'd make it to his car unscathed, but he did. When he started it up, he thought surely they would come for him then. They wouldn't let him hit the road with the diamonds. But that's just what he did. He kept his eyes on the rearview and side mirrors as he drove and did not spot a tail. For the first fifteen minutes, he did not drive to his destination. He made indiscriminate turns, hopping on the freeway and then off again, knowing no one could keep up with him without revealing themselves.

Not until he was positive that he didn't have a tail did he make the first of a few stops. He dropped the tracker off at a vacant house on the south side. He concealed it in the shrubbery next to the front porch. He then booked it back to the west side, where he owned another home. This one was one story, three bedrooms, two baths. He planned to use it as a rental property once everything settled down. For now, it was a convenient place to stash both the SUV and the diamonds.

He left the house on foot, bringing nothing but his suitcase. As he rolled it down the sidewalk, he considered the possibility that Rat may very well have been working alone. That would be the best case scenario, but he refused to rely on such fortune.

It took him ten minutes to walk out of the neighborhood and to a modest shopping center. Once there, he used his phone to request an Uber. He gave the address of a car rental company as his destination.

Forty-five minutes later, he was behind the wheel again. His new ride was an Infiniti QX80. It was super clean and smelled brand new, even though there were 40,000 miles on the dash. Lola had texted him again since he left the hotel. He took this opportunity to call her back.

"Hello," She answered. "Is everything okay? Where are you?"

"I'm on my way back to the hotel," he told her. "Sorry I didn't call sooner. I had to concentrate on my driving, make sure no one was following me."

"You got the diamonds? They were still there?"

"Yeah. I got 'em. I didn't see anyone waiting for me. I think we might be good, but I wanna give it awhile, just to be sure."

"Okay," she breathed. "How far away are you? When will you get here?"

Her compassion warmed his heart, though he knew she was only reacting to their dire straits. Her concern probably didn't mean their friendship was on the mend. But it felt good to hear it, just the same.

"I'm twenty minutes away," he said. "I won't be long."

"Okay," she said. "Be careful."

"Thanks. I will."

CHAPTER SEVEN
SECOND DATE

Mediating
On this mess gives me a migraine
These missing brains and shitty stains
All these remains, glazed and strained
Filleted, displayed in slashing rain
Why should we love when we can hate?
Build 'em up when we can rape?
Why should we ask when we can take?
Clear 'em out and clean the slate
This is the life we choose to live
Can't stop it now, this train is rolling
This train is going, faster now
Spitting sparks. This bitch is stolen

Once again, Lola was surprised by the fullness in her heart when Von returned to their hotel room. The emotion was pleasant, so she didn't try to suppress it. But she did resist the urge to rise from her seat and embrace him as he crossed the threshold with a cute and accomplished smile on his face.

"You had me worried about you," she said, "when you didn't respond to my texts."

"I know. I'm sorry."

Drawn to the smell of cooked food, he left his suitcase by the sofa and headed to the coffee table where he found two covered plates.

"I got lunch for you," she said. "I didn't know what you wanted, so I got the same thing I had – beef teriyaki."

"I'm so hungry, I can eat a Billy goat," he replied. "Let me take a shower first." He changed direction and headed for the bedrooms.

"Alright. I'll heat it up for you when you get back."

Fifteen minutes later, he sat at a small table and dug into his meal. While he ate, he told her what he'd been up to. Lola remained on the sofa, once again enthralled by his story. She found him intriguing on their first date. Now that he was being honest, she realized his life was much more thrilling and complex. He was like a character from a Jason Bourne movie. She had a few follow-up questions when he was done speaking.

"I can't believe you have all those diamonds," she breathed. "I wanted you to get them, but now, it feels like we're in even more danger."

"I agree. I don't think we're out of the woods yet."

"What's your plan for them? You said Saul was worried that you wouldn't be able to sell them."

"He's right. It is risky. But I've only been working with Saul for a few years. Before that, I was on my own. I have contacts on the black market. That's why I came back home. I know people in this area who can help me out. If they don't want the diamonds for themselves, they can put me in contact with people who can afford them."

"What about the tracker? Why didn't you just throw it away?"

"I have to go back for it," he said. "That's the second part of my plan. If Rat was working alone, we'd be good. But he said he told Saul about our plan. If Saul knows about the tracker, more people will come looking for it."

"But without the tracker, they can't find you. Isn't that what you want?"

He shook his head. "If I go that route, I'll be looking over my shoulder for the rest of my life. I didn't go through all of this to be on the run indefinitely. The only way to know I'm safe is to eliminate all threats. I know that's not something you want to hear, but I have to do that – for you too. I know you wanna go home, but if Rat was in touch with Saul the whole time he was down here, your house still isn't safe. I have to know for sure."

With that, Lola's sense of dread returned. She didn't find any flaws in Von's logic. But still, she wished there was some other way.

She asked him, "How will you use the tracker to find out if someone else is after us?"

"I have to get it and expose myself," he said matter-of-factly. "That's how it worked with Rat, and I wasn't even looking for him this morning. Next time, I'll be more vigilant. I'll get them before they have a chance to do something to me."

"Like human bait? That's your plan?"

"Not exactly. I don't plan to walk around with the tracker in my pocket. I wanna go somewhere where there's a lot of people and put the tracker in a place where I can keep an eye on it. If someone makes a move, then I'll know who or what I'm dealing with."

"And if someone does go for the tracker, you want to eliminate them," she said, "that means kill them…"

He stopped eating and turned so he could stare into her large, brown eyes. "I know how you feel about that. I promise I won't get you caught up again. It won't be like how it happened with Rat."

She nodded, her eyes glazed. She was watching him, but Von didn't feel like she was looking at him anymore. "Your brother," he guessed. "Can you tell me what happened to him? I understand, if you don't wanna talk about it."

Her eyes regained focus on his. She hesitated for so long, he didn't think she'd respond, but finally she said, "Yeah. Okay. It's, um, it's a lot more than what I said before. My brother, he, um… The day he was killed, I killed somebody too. I don't – I don't think I've ever really talked about it, not after I left the police station…"

Stunned, Von left his seat and sat on the sofa next to her. Lola brought her hands to her lap and stared down at them as she began speaking.

"My brother, he was a good guy. A real good dude. I'm not just saying that 'cause I'm his sister. Everybody liked him. He was always popular. He made some bad decisions, but he didn't deserve what happened to him."

Von asked her, "What was his name?" his tone comforting.

"Ricky. He was my only sibling. He was never really into school. After graduating, he decided college wasn't his thing. Didn't want to go to the military, or nothing like that. He just started working. After a couple of years, he got on with Amazon. I thought it was a good job, working in the warehouse. I mean, it was shit work, but he had leadership skills. I thought he could work his way up to a better position, if he kept showing up on time and doing his best.

"But Ricky hated that job. He had some friends from high school that he still hung out with. They were into selling drugs. Mostly weed, but they sold pills too. Fentanyl, I think. When I found out Ricky was wrapped up in it, I was disappointed. I gave him the talk. Nagged him sometimes. I even cut him off for a few months. But after a while, you know, I just accepted it. I figured it was his life, you know. I wish I didn't give up so easily."

Her eyes were watery, but the tears didn't spill. She swallowed and shook her head slowly.

"The day he died, I was riding with him. He picked me up to go with him to look at a motorcycle he was thinking about buying – wanted me to drive his car home, if he decided to get it. He had ten thousand in cash, saved it from whatever he was selling. I remember telling him he was stupid for rolling around with all that money. He told me he was good. He reached over and popped the glove compartment open. Showed me a gun he had in there. My dad, he kept a gun in the house. I never messed with it – outside of the one time he took me out to the country and showed me how to shoot it when I turned eighteen.

"I didn't know my brother was rolling like that, selling drugs and packing heat. Made me look at him different. If I had more time with him, I planned to try again, maybe have an intervention or something to get him to change his lifestyle. But that was the last time I was with him. He stopped at a corner store to get some cigarettes. When he came out, he had this weird look on his face. He got his gun out the glove compartment. He was nervous, said he saw some guys, and they were looking at him funny.

"I didn't have time to look around for whoever he was talking about. I was more shocked that he took his gun out and cocked it. He put it in his lap and started his car. Before he could back out, somebody ran up to us. A black man stuck a gun in the window. He said, '*Give it up.*' Just like that. Everything was going so fast. I'm staring at this gun. This man. He didn't have a mask. He looked *normal.* Like anybody. And then he looked down, and he yelled, '*He got a gun!*' And then he started shooting."

Lola squeezed her eyes closed, and the tears began to flow. Her head rolled back, and she sucked in a long, deep breath. She was now wringing her hands in her lap. Von was torn. He wanted to reach for her hands. He wanted to wrap an arm around her. He didn't know if she'd be receptive to either gesture, so he remained still. She opened her eyes but didn't look his way. She stared straight ahead, her mind's eye replaying a scene far away from the hotel room.

"I saw him get shot," she said. "I didn't see where he was shot, but I saw his body jump. I saw the blood. I heard him scream. The man shot again, and then he reached in the car. He was reaching for my brother's gun. I think. I don't know. It was all going so fast, but at the same time, it kinda felt like slow motion. I don't know what it was in me that made me react the way I did, but I grabbed the gun before he got to it. I grabbed it, and I pointed it out the window, and I started shooting. It was so loud. The gun kicked so hard, I almost dropped it. But whatever gave me the speed to get to it so fast also gave me the strength to hold on to it.

"I don't know how many times I shot. All I know is when it was over, and everything quieted down, I could hear my brother. He wasn't screaming anymore. He was breathing, but I could tell it hurt him to breathe. He was breathing so hard. He was trying to breathe. His eyes were wide open. He looked so scared. I was crying. Begging him not to die. Begging him to hold on. I didn't know what to do. When he stopped breathing, I felt like it was my fault, because I didn't know what to do, so I didn't do anything. But I found out, later I found out I couldn't have done anything. He got shot in the chest. One of the arteries in his heart. Even if he was in a hospital, nobody could have saved him."

Von remained quiet. He wanted to say something, but he understood the importance of allowing Lola to speak her piece. There was a reason she wanted to share this story with him at this moment. He felt that she had not yet revealed the reason.

"I didn't think I hit anybody when I was shooting, but it turns out I shot a kid."

Von could not stop his mouth from falling open. He was glad she wasn't watching him and didn't see his shocked expression.

"It wasn't your fault," he said.

"Yeah." She swallowed, nodding. "That's what the police said. They arrested the guy who tried to rob us. Turns out he knew some of my brother's friends. My brother actually met his killer, but I don't know if he was paying any attention to him at the time. He was so happy about buying that bike. Before he picked me up, he was kicking it with some of his homeboys. He told them he was getting a bike that day. Told them he was paying cash. The guy who tried to rob us, his name is Roderick; he was there at the time.

"He followed my brother when he left his friend's apartment. Followed him to my apartment when he picked me up. Roderick was on the phone with some other guys, letting them know where we were headed, what streets we were on. When we stopped at the store, they pulled in right behind us. The way the law works in Texas is if you're committing a crime, and somebody gets killed, you're responsible for their death. I think they put that law in place for the police, you know, like if they shooting at a bank robber, and they hit a bystander. But the law works for everybody. Roderick and the two guys he brought with him got charged for both murders – my brother and the little boy I shot."

Von's heart bled for her. No one should have to carry such a burden.

He asked her, "How old was the boy?"

"Eleven. Desmond Green. That's his name. That was his name."

Her tears continued to fall like blood.

"That–" She took a shuddering breath. "That's, um, that's why I don't like to be around guns. When you came to my house and Rat was there..."

"I get it," Von said. "I understand. It was my fault. I was so focused on how I wanted things to go, I didn't consider how something like that would affect you. It wasn't fair, to put you through that."

She met his eye then. She asked him, "Do you think, once all of this is said and done, you could give me something – not that much – for me to give to Desmond's family? I know money won't make things better. And it's been a long time. Almost twenty years. But I know his family is poor, and I think they deserve..." She trailed off. "I don't know..."

Von agreed that money would not heal wounds, but it could make things a little better. It could move Desmond's family out of the hood. And it could provide a bit of the closure Lola desperately needed.

"It's not a problem," he said. "Whatever you want. We can do that."

"Thank you."

She surprised him by reaching to squeeze his hand.

"I'ma go lay down for a while," she said as she rose to her feet.

Von didn't like the idea of her being alone after reliving such haunting memories, but he knew she didn't want him to come to her bedroom.

"Okay," he said. "I'm gonna take off after a while. I won't wake you, if you're asleep."

∞ ∞ ∞ ∞ ∞ ∞ ∞

Von left his bedroom at 8 p.m. wearing jeans with a Polo golf shirt and sneakers. It felt good to be clean and freshly groomed. Despite all that had occurred that day, he was alert and only mildly anxious about what he planned to do that night. He went to check on Lola before he left the hotel. Her door was open. She was lying on the bed, with her back to him. She was still dressed and hadn't pulled the sheets over her.

"Hey, you awake?" he said, not too loudly.

She rolled in his direction, and he saw that she hadn't been asleep.

"Yeah," she said.

She looked a lot better than the last time he spoke to her. He knew that sometimes having an attentive ear to listen to a repressed memory could be therapeutic, even if the listener doesn't provide counseling.

She looked him up and down and said, "You look good."

"Thank you."

She sat up and then swung her legs over the bed. "Where you going?"

"To a carnival."

Her eyes narrowed at that.

"There's a carnival tonight in Fossil Creek," he explained, referring to an affluent neighborhood in Overbrook Meadows' north side. "It's an annual spring celebration. I think this will be a good place to draw out anyone else who might be looking for me."

She remembered what he told her about seeking out a public area for the next phase of his plan. But she wondered, "How do you plan to eliminate the threat, with so many people around?"

"Don't worry, I'm prepared for whatever I may encounter."

She continued to frown at him.

"Don't look at me like that," he said with a chuckle. "I'm not gonna shoot up a carnival, if that's what you're thinking. Most of what I do is more subtle. What happened with Rat, that was not how I normally handle things."

She nodded. The worry lines on her forehead melted away. "Can I go?" she asked.

Now it was Von's turn to appear confused. "Why would you want to do that? I'm trying to keep you *away* from danger."

"You don't think you'll need my help?"

"No," he said honestly.

"Well, damn."

"I'm not trying to be mean." He continued to smile at her.

"You think I'd get in your way?"

"No. I guess it would be good to have some company. I just don't want to do anything that would make you uncomfortable."

"I'm not as weak as you think."

"I know. I never said that."

"Aren't we in this together? You said they would come after me, if they can't get to you."

"Yeah, but... You know what, maybe you should come. I doubt if anything will pop off tonight. If not, this will give me an opportunity to take you out again. I asked you to go on a second date, but that didn't work out."

"No, it didn't," she said with a smirk. "You said you were taking me to the Botanical Gardens. Instead, you took me to a nasty duck pond and dumped a body."

His eyes widened. "Okay. Tell me how you really feel."

"I was gonna tell you that earlier," she said, grinning. "But it wasn't a good time to crack a joke."

Chuckling, he said, "I'm glad to see you're feeling good enough to find humor in some of this. I was starting to worry that I stole your joy – permanently."

"Nah." She pushed off the bed and headed for her suitcase. "Should I change?"

"I think you look good," he replied, "but you can, if you want to."

"Can you give me about ten minutes, or are you in a hurry?"

"No, take your time. The carnival is open 'til eleven. I'll wait for you in the living room. You want me to close your door?" he asked as he backed out of the room.

"Yeah. I won't be that long."

Von closed the door and made his way to the living room sofa. He took a seat, a bewildered smile on his face. Lola had more layers than an extravagant wedding cake. His mind was flooded with scenarios that all started with the word *Maybe*. He shut all of these thoughts down. The only maybe that mattered was whether he could sell the diamonds and move on with his life with no threats from his past. It was better to focus on that, rather than emotional intangibles.

CHAPTER EIGHT
EPINEPHRINE

Hot caramel scents
Hoover like hummingbirds
And water the tongues of children
Who smile with toothy grins
Free from sin
They cling to the hems of their mother's dresses
And they are precious
And they are blessed
And cotton candy is swirled
Into huge pink and blue clouds
It electrifies the crowd that gathers 'round
And the sounds of games and fun
Seem to be on one mind and one accord
Though scattered and diverse
Everyone litters, but no one is reprimanded
Excitement is even-handed
And no one is demanding
And young lovers hold hands
As they streak for the rides
The Ferris wheel that takes them high
So high that no one can see them and insist
That they stop

ONE NIGHT STAND

When they kiss
It's like fireworks
In their minds
That makes them blind

Before heading to the carnival, Von made a couple of stops. The first was at property #2, where he'd stashed the diamonds and the Tahoe. He went inside and returned to the Infiniti with what appeared to be a toy gun, but Lola doubted if that was the case. After what happened to Rat, she knew that the game they were playing was deadly serious.

"It's a tranquilizer dart gun," Von told her. "I told you I wasn't gon' shoot up a carnival."

"So, if someone gives us trouble, you plan to put them to sleep? How is that helpful?"

He shot her a grin. "Okay, Doubting Thomas. I keep telling you, I got a plan. But don't worry about it. I'm starting to think Rat was the only one searching for the tracker. We'll know for sure after tonight."

Von's second stop was at a vacant house on the south side. Lola watched him curiously as he exited the vehicle, made his way to the front porch, and then knelt to retrieve something from the bushes. He got back in the rental and showed her the GPS Tracker.

"We gotta be careful now," he said, looking around. "Someone might have eyes on us from this moment on..."

Lola's skin prickled as she joined Von in surveying their environment. It was dark, and there were a few people moving about. It didn't look as though anyone was watching them, but it was impossible to tell.

"The fact that it was still there makes me feel better about our chances," he mused. "If someone tracked it all the way from California, why would they make it this far and not take it with them?"

"California, is that were your last job was?"

He nodded. "That's where Saul lives, too."

"Maybe they couldn't find it," Lola offered. "It's pretty small, and it's black."

"Maybe," Von agreed. He turned left on the next street and headed for the highway. He continued to check his mirrors, as he'd done when Rat was following them. "But if it was me," he said, "I would've dug up the whole bush until I found it. We're talking fifteen million worth of diamonds. That's not something I'd give up on so easily."

Lola agreed with that assertion. She didn't respond.

∞ ∞ ∞ ∞ ∞ ∞ ∞

The Fossil Creek Spring Carnival was a week-long celebration that coincided with Overbrook Meadows' school district's spring break. This was the last night of the festivities. Over three thousand locals had come out to partake in the family fun. Von paid the admission for Lola and himself, and they were immediately engulfed in the crowd, the lights, the sounds of rides and excited voices, the smell of hot dogs and corn dogs, funnel cakes and burgers, turkey legs, popcorn and fried Oreos.

Lola understood this was a mission, and the stakes were high, but she couldn't stop an eager smile from lighting her features as she took in their surroundings. In the distance she saw a Ferris wheel, its beautiful lights twinkling in the night sky. Ahead of them, carnies shouted at passerby's, enticing them to try their luck with a ring toss or a basketball game that featured hoops that were not much bigger than the balls. Von moved in that direction. He took Lola's hand in his as they walked. She did not pull away.

"This is for show," he said. "We're pretending to be a couple on a second date."

"*Sure*. Any excuse to try to get back on my good side."

He looked her way and saw that she was grinning. He shot her a wink and led her deeper into the carnival games. They smiled but didn't stop for any of the con artists who offered stuffed animals that could be purchased at Walmart for five or ten dollars in return for attempts at contests that looked simple but were anything but.

Von finally stopped at a whiffle ball toss. This game was also a scam, but at least there was a chance of one of the very bouncing balls landing in one of the colored holes, rather than bouncing off the table completely.

"How much?" he asked the game booth operator.

"Three balls for ten dollars," she said. "You played this game before?"

"No," Von said as he dug the money from his pocket. "And I don't plan to try tonight. I'ma let my lady have a shot."

Lola was surprised to hear that. "Why me? I suck at all of these games."

"It's okay," Von said. "I'ma look around for a minute. When I get back, you better have won one of those unicorns."

She played along and took the balls from the woman.

"Good luck!" the lady said.

"We'll see," Lola replied.

In less than a minute, she'd burned through ten dollars' worth of balls, and Von returned to her side.

"How'd you do?" he asked.

She shook her head wistfully. "I think you already know the answer to that."

As they walked away, she asked him, "Where'd you go?"

"I hid the tracker in one of the games, the one with the water guns. It's back there with the attendant. He didn't see me toss it on the ground next to him."

"Does that mean you won't be able to get it back?"

"Yeah. And if someone tracks it to this location, they won't be able to get to it either. I'm guessing they'll be walking around the area for a long time, trying to figure out why a carnie has those diamonds. Should make them pretty conspicuous."

Lola agreed that it would. She liked his plan.

"We'll stay 'til they close at eleven," he said. "We don't have to stay in this area the whole time, but we should check on it regularly."

"If they can't get to it with so many people around," Lola surmised, "They'll probably hang back, until everyone starts to leave. Maybe they'll try to wait the attendant out, so they can try to get to the tag."

"Maybe," Von said. "Or maybe no one will show at all. Time will tell."

"Okay."

"You feel like riding anything?"

Her eyes twinkled. "Yeah. The Ferris wheel."

"I'm more drawn to the Fireball," Von said, looking in the direction of the large, one-track circle, the only ride at the carnival that offered thrill seekers the opportunity for loop-the-loops.

"How'd I know you'd be interested in something like that?"

"My life is all about risks," he said. "But I've been thinking about settling down."

She looked into his eyes. "Hmmm. Have you really?"

"Yeah. In more ways than one."

"Are you flirting with me, or are we still playing a role?"

"So many questions..."

"Okay, just one more."

"Shoot."

"Can you buy me a funnel cake?"

He took her hand again and led her towards a concession booth. "Yeah, girl. Let's get you a funnel cake."

∞ ∞ ∞ ∞ ∞ ∞ ∞

Despite the weirdness of everything that was going on, Lola would be lying if she said she didn't begin to enjoy her second date with Von – only it wasn't a real date (they were just faking it), but it sure felt like the real thing. Von felt the same way. As the Ferris wheel whipped them high in the air, and the lights from the carnival reflected off the moon, shone back to earth, and glistened in Lola's eyes, the strong feelings he felt during their first date returned.

At Del Frisco's, he had found her company delightful. She didn't have an exciting lifestyle, definitely not compared to his, but that wasn't what sparked the attraction when he first ran into her at the bank. To him, she was beautiful, her buttery skin tone, the spark in her eyes when she smiled at him the first time. And their first night together. So many unexpected erotic pleasures. He didn't deserve a woman who fulfilled him so completely. He'd be the first to admit that.

After what happened with Rat, he thought he would never have the fortune of seeing her smile at him again. But here they were. He dared to wish that this night could go on forever.

Unfortunately, good times, it seemed, never do.

He spotted her as the Ferris wheel made its final rotation and began to slow. He couldn't miss her. Katrina was a natural redhead. She was smart enough to cover most of her distinctive colorful mane with a baseball cap, but the red hair flowing from beneath the hat, coupled with her almost freakishly pale skin was a dead giveaway. Were he in her shoes, Von would've opted for a wig or possibly a dye job, but he understood that this type of mission was not Katrina's expertise. In their crew, which had pilfered fifteen million dollars' worth of diamonds in one haul, the redhead was the safe cracker. She was accomplished and confident when stealthily infiltrating a target's home. In this setting, however, she was out of her league.

Von kept his eyes on her as the Ferris wheel came to a stop, and he and Lola disembarked. Katrina scanned the area and then turned, looking in another direction. Von thought she had seen them, but while seated in the Ferris wheel, the metal portion of their passenger car was almost chest high. The glass from the top portion may have created a glare and obscured them further.

Katrina began to walk away from them, no more than thirty yards away. Within a few seconds, she was almost lost in the crowd. Von was eager to unbuckle his safety belt and follow her. When their feet returned to solid ground, he took hold of Lola's hand and led her away from the ride, towards the middle of the fairground.

He told her, "We got company."

Lola's smile froze and then slipped off her face. She wasn't surprised to hear this, but a part of her had begun to hope that the gruesome business with Rat was the last of it. She'd begun to think that she and Von would leave the carnival and stop somewhere nice for a late dinner. And in a few days, Von would sell the diamonds, and as impractical as it all sounded, now that she was thinking about it, they'd live happily ever after.

"Who is it?" she asked, her mouth dry, her eyes scanning the crowd for a face she wouldn't recognize if she ran right into it.

"It's Katrina," Von said, his voice casual, almost implausibly so. "I saw her when we were on the Ferris wheel. She's up there, headed towards the main area, back to where I left the tracker. I don't think she saw us."

Don't think? Lola found that terribly insufficient.

"What are we gonna do?"

"For now, follow her. You know I always got a plan..."

But that plan began to fall through as the crowd became denser, and it became more difficult to pursue their pursuer. From the Ferris wheels' elevated platform, it had been easy to spot Katrina's blue ball cap and flagrant red hair. But at ground level, he was not able to overcome the lead she had on them. When they reached the carnival game area, he looked around, in all directions, and realized he had lost sight of her.

"Shit," he murmured.

"What's wrong?"

"I lost her."

Lola began to look around, a subconscious effort of futility. "What does she look like?"

"She's a redhead," Von said, "wearing a blue cap. Jeans and a tee-shirt. But don't look for her. If she's watching us, I don't want her to know that we know she's here."

They continued walking through the maze of carnival games. It was nearly impossible to heed Von's warning and not scan the area. Lola wanted to look over her shoulder so badly her neck grew stiff with the effort it took her to fight against it. They marched on, ignoring the carnies and excited screams of the children.

Unexpectedly, Von told her, "Let's go this way."

He made a right between the ring toss and basketball game. Lola followed.

He told her, "Don't look back, but she's on us. I saw her out of the corner of my eye. I thought I was gonna get to her first, but she's better than I thought. Prolly been stalking us the whole time."

The hairs stood on the back of Lola's neck, now that she knew for sure that their adversary was watching them.

"So, what now?" she asked. Keeping her voice level required a good deal of effort.

"A little tricky now," he acknowledged. "I think I can still pull this off if I can…" His eyes flashed. "Yeah, that'll work."

Lola followed his gaze. She didn't see anything ahead of them except more of the carnival.

"What?" she asked. "What do you see?"

"The fun house," he said. "House of mirrors. When we get inside, you have to do exactly as I say. You have to trust me."

She felt like he'd told her that a thousand times. Those words never made her feel comfortable before, and they didn't now.

"Trust you with what?" Her eyes were wide, but not yet panicked. "What do you want me to do?"

"We're going in there," Von said. He didn't hurry towards the attraction, but his pace was steady and deliberate. "I've always been good with figuring out these things. It's like a maze, made more complicated with the mirrors, but there's a pattern to it."

"You've been to *this* carnival? They're all different, aren't they?"

"No, I haven't been here. Even though they're all different, they're pretty much the same. It's just a maze. Once you get past the mirrors, it's not hard to make it to the other side."

Get past the mirrors? As if that was an easy task.

"Your plan is to go in there?"

He nodded. "Yeah."

"And then what?"

"And then we make it out before her. If she's smart, she'll wait for us to come out. But I'm betting she'll follow us in. If she can get close enough, that'll give her the privacy to do what she came here to do."

"And what's that?"

"I can't say. Killing me won't get the diamonds back, but maybe she's so pissed, that's what she wants at this point."

Lola felt like he was leading them into a trap, but Von was supremely confident in his decision. They approached the vendor and provided the necessary tickets to enter the attraction. Lola was unsure of her steps and her surroundings the moment they stepped inside. In every direction she looked, she saw a reflection of her and Von. His expression was deathly serious. Her eyes revealed that she expected the worst.

She willed herself to get it together. She could've been waiting for him comfortably and safely in the hotel room. He wanted to leave her there. She was the one who asked to tag along. She knew the perils that faced them, and she had trusted him to keep her safe. She understood that it was crucial for her to continue to trust him now.

He gripped her hand and immediately began to move forward through the maze. Ahead of them, they heard voices. Three, maybe four people were completely dumbfounded. Laughing, one of them shouted that they were definitely going in circles. Von continued to move, pulling Lola along, making rights and then lefts with no discernable rhyme or reason. But his feet were sure, his pace quickened. At every turn, she watched his eyes in the mirror. His head moved left, then right, and then he made a decision.

Minutes passed. Lola would swear it was more like hours. They passed the group ahead of them that had proclaimed they were stumped. They passed another couple who were all smiles, even though they were equally confused. How many turns had Von made? Were they going in circles? Were they lost as well? But just when doubt began to take hold and dig it's claws into the back of her neck, Von made the last turn and rushed towards what he believed to be the exit. A moment later, they were reunited with the night sky. They had made it. Lola sighed with relief, but Von was even more focused now.

"Go in there," he said, pointing towards a gift shop. "Wait for me. I'm going back through." Looking around, he said, "She's not out here waiting for us. That means she followed us inside. I'm going in after her."

"You think it's a good idea to go back in there?"

"Yes. Wait for me in the gift shop. I won't be long."

Although she thought this plan was sketchy at best, Lola didn't advise against it. She'd been wrong about this man too many times to count.

She simply said, "Okay."

Her mind was so disjointed from her body, she didn't feel the muscles in her legs contract as they propelled her to the gift shop.

∞ ∞ ∞ ∞ ∞ ∞ ∞

Back at the entrance of the Fun House of Mirrors, Von hurriedly handed three more tickets to the attendant.

"Wow. You got through that so fast!" she said. "You wanna go again?"

"Yeah. It was fun. Wanna see if I can beat my record."

"Where's your girlfriend? She's not coming this time?"

"No, she's gonna sit this one out," he said and walked inside.

"Good luck!" the girl called after him.

During his first trip through the maze, Von memorized the layout, much like he did with the houses he and his crew planned to burglarize. He was cautious but no less speedy as he made the same turns and avoided the dead ends that looked like turns because of the bewildering reflections.

Halfway through the funhouse, he spotted Katrina's blue ballcap. He was relieved that his assumption was correct; she had followed them inside but wasn't able to make it out as easily as he and Lola had. His next emotion was trepidation. If he got too close, she would see him in the reflections. He didn't know what she had in mind, following him into this maze. If she planned to kill him outright and be done with it, that wouldn't be hard to accomplish in these cramped, confusing hallways.

He hung back, not too far. Far enough to give him the advantage she had so foolishly relinquished. Close enough to see Katrina when she made a left turn, although the only route to the exit was on her right. Von made his move then. Although he hadn't studied the route she'd taken, he suspected it would lead to a dead end. He drew his weapon and hurried to cut her off. He barely made it. The corridor she turned on was only ten feet long. When she reached the end of it, she came face to face with her reflection, as she had countless other times in the maze. But this time, she saw a familiar face standing behind her.

Stunned, she whipped around with the speed of a snake, but it was too late.

Von pulled the trigger and hit her dead center with a tranquilizer dart. She yelped in shock and pain, no doubt thinking that she'd been struck by a bullet. Eyes wide, she stared at Von in disbelief and gripped her midsection. She first felt and then looked down at the foreign object. She yanked the dart from her abdomen and eyed it quizzically. When she looked up again, Von was gone.

∞ ∞ ∞ ∞ ∞ ∞ ∞

He and Lola waited near the gift shop, for what felt like an interminable amount of time.

"Are you sure she'll make it out?" Lola wondered aloud.

"I hope so," Von muttered. "Otherwise, I'll have to go back in there *again*."

"Why didn't you kill her when you had the chance?" Lola breathed.

He was surprised to hear her say that.

"I want to make it look like an accident," he explained. "With all these people around, I thought…"

He trailed off as the object of their curiosity finally emerged from the funhouse exit. Compared to the last time he'd seen her, Katrina was a lot worse for wear. Her dazed expression was matched by her unsteady gait.

"*Shit…*" Lola's heart thundered. "Is she okay?"

Before Von could respond, they watched as Katrina stumbled forward and supported herself with the help of a trash bin. A few onlookers noticed her stumble and moved to assist her. That was Von's cue.

"Wait here," he told Lola. "I'll be back."

He walked quickly and deliberately to his old friend. In one hand, he palmed his second weapon. By the time he made it to her, the Good Samaritans had helped Katrina to a seated position, and they were calling for help. There were ten people surrounding her now. More were on the way.

Von pushed through them asking, "What's wrong with her? What happened?"

Katrina's eyes blazed at him, but none of her other muscles worked as she intended them to, not even her voice. She muttered something. Her eyes were half closed. Gravity pulled her further down onto the pavement. She wasn't strong enough to resist.

She was fully on her back now. The tranquilizer Von hit her with could take down a bear. Katrina was only 150 pounds fully clothed.

"Wait," he told the crowd. "Let me through."

The eyes on him registered confusion and concern.

"She's saying something," Von said. He knelt next to the fallen body and lowered his face until his ear was so close to her lips, he could feel her breaths. Katrina's lips were still moving. This was extremely beneficial.

"*EpiPen!*" he announced to the crowd. "She's having an allergic reaction. She said she needs her EpiPen!"

Half of the onlookers offered helpful advice. Von ignored all of them. He looked around and then began to rummage through the crossbody purse Katrina toted. He pretended not to notice the gun she had in there – the one she undoubtedly planned to use on him – and emerged with the EpiPen he had already palmed. His sleight of hand was so impressive, David Copperfield would've been proud.

"*I found it!*" he declared. "My cousin is allergic to peanuts. I know how to use one of these."

Katrina began to protest with everything she had in her. Whatever she was trying to do with her voice and her limbs was blocked by the tranquilizer's effects, but this was just as good. Her jerky motions made her look like she was on the verge of a seizure.

Before anyone could stop him, Von stabbed the injector into her thigh. Katrina began to fight against the fog even harder. It was a spectacular show. Von stood, just as the event security made it to the scene. With all eyes on the downed woman, it was easy to slip his EpiPen into his back pocket and remove a real EpiPen from his other pocket.

"I think she's having a seizure," Von told one of the staff members. "Here." He handed him the EpiPen. "I found this in her purse. I gave her the shot. I think she's gonna be okay…"

The man took the injector from him and then knelt to check on Katrina. The other security guard reached for his radio and delivered an urgent message to whoever was listening on the other end. No one, not even the onlookers, were watching Von as he backed away and then walked to where he'd left Lola.

He grabbed her hand and said, "Come on."

She couldn't help but stare back at the spectacle as he pulled her away.

Finally, she looked Von's way and asked, "*What happened? What'd you do?*"

Von didn't respond. He was doing something with his hands. She looked down and saw him removing something from his fingers. She had never seen finger tip protectors before, but immediately she knew what they were. Each one rolled off his digits like a miniature condom. She was surprised that he'd found a set that matched his skin tone.

"We gotta get out of here," he said, leading her to the carnival exit.

"She had an EpiPen?" Lola asked. Even she was surprised by how calm she was.

"Nope," Von said. "The one I gave them is a real EpiPen. But the one in my pocket, it was full of poison. It's only a matter of time now…"

CHAPTER NINE
MARVEL

Back in the Infiniti, they drove slowly through the crowded parking lot. Von checked his surroundings, thinking a staff member would stop them before they exited the fairgrounds. But that didn't happen. They rolled out of the parking lot and merged with the traffic on the main thoroughfare. Five minutes later, they were booking it down the freeway.

By then, Lola had calmed her nerves sufficiently. Her voice was surprisingly calm when she asked, "What's gonna happen to her?"

"She'll be dead before we make it back to the hotel," he said matter-of-factly.

"You used the tranquilizer on her, in the funhouse?"

He nodded. "I planned to use it out in the open. But the funhouse, I didn't plan for that. It was perfect though; the tranquilizer gun was louder than I thought. A lot of people would have heard it, if I used it in a crowd."

"And the EpiPen, you had all of that planned too?"

"Yeah. I knew there'd be security at the fair. Some cops too, working the event. If she dropped dead, and it was obviously a murder, I don't think we would've made it out of there as easily as we did."

"How'd you get poison in an EpiPen?" she wondered.

"Took me a while to come up with that. Never tried it before. I'm always looking for non-lethal ways to get what I want. I'll kill if I have to, but it's not my go-to. The poison in the injector isn't untraceable, but it would take a full toxicology report to find it in her system. If she's still alive when she makes it to the hospital, they might do testing like that. But, like I told you, the timer on her expiration date started ticking the moment I gave her the shot." He checked the phone on the Infiniti's dashboard. "She's got about five minutes left, tops."

Lola's eyes narrowed. She shook her head in bewilderment. "How do you – I don't... I don't understand how you could've planned something so elaborate. And it all worked out, exactly how you wanted it to."

"Planning, it's... That's what I do. I told you I started off small-time. As my targets got bigger, so did the risks. A house like yours probably has ADT. I figured out how to hack into those systems before I hooked up with Saul. The security systems at the mansions we've been hitting, those are state of the art. It takes some Ocean's Eleven type of planning to get into those places. That's where my expertise comes in. I have to be prepared for every eventuality before I even think about stepping foot onto someone's property."

Lola considered her next words before speaking. "I wanna believe you're not a stone cold killer. After what happened to Rat, you said that's not how you normally handle things. But tonight, you made it look so easy. I mean, I know there was nothing easy about what you did, but…"

"I get what you're saying." He sighed. "Look, whenever something is planned to the T, it looks easier than it actually is. But as far as murder, I was being honest when I said that's not something I do on a regular basis. I have taken lives, from time to time, but not like you're thinking – not like the way you're looking at me."

Lola wasn't aware of the way she was looking at him, but his *from time to time* comment made her feel that whatever vibes she was putting off were justified.

"How many people have you killed?" she asked directly.

After a sigh, he said, "Counting Rat and Katrina, six."

"They were all bad guys, who were trying to kill you?"

Another pause and another sigh. Lola took that as a sign that he was about to be deceitful, but he said, "Can we talk about this when we get back to the room? I think Katrina might be the end of it, but I'm trying to concentrate on my driving; need to make sure no one's following us."

Likely excuse, she thought. She also considered asking him to get a separate room for her. He could certainly afford it.

But then Von added, "If you want me to talk about some heavy shit like that, I need a drink first."

Lola accepted that and quieted down for the remainder of the ride.

∞ ∞ ∞ ∞ ∞ ∞ ∞

In all the hotels she'd had the pleasure of patronizing, partaking in the alcohol provided in the mini fridge was taboo for Lola. But Von was a different animal. He was pleased to find small bottles of vodka, rum and tequila. He grabbed six of them and took them to the dining room table, where Lola had taken a seat on the sofa.

"There's some Coke in there too," Von said. "But I'm drinking mine straight."

Two days ago, Lola would've sent him back for the coke. But she selected a little bottle of tequila and told him, "That's okay. I'm good with this."

They both twisted the tops off their bottles and took a swig. Von took a manly gulp, nearly finishing his. Lola only had one swallow.

"It's bad enough you caught up with a thief," Von said, reading her mind. "Now you wondering what other evils I'm capable of."

He sat back on the sofa, looking at her. He gave her a little space, but he was still within arm's reach.

When she didn't respond, he said, "I wanna preface this by saying that when you're in a certain lifestyle, there are things that come with it that go against what the average law-abiding citizen would understand or be comfortable with. Not making excuses for anything I've done, but we come from two different worlds. Our moral compasses will probably never be aligned."

Lola understood that. Again, she remained silent.

"The first one," he said, "was a guy I got hooked up with back when I was getting started. In those days, I preferred to work alone, but I learned there's strength in numbers. The last crew I was with proved that. They were all professionals. I couldn't have done any of those jobs without them. But finding someone you can trust with your life and your freedom, that's always gonna be hit or miss.

"The first guy, his name was Benny. He had just got out of prison for burglary. I was nineteen at the time. He was fifteen years older than me. I looked at him like a veteran. He knew way more about the business than I did. I learned a lot from him, and I trusted him. I never thought he would burn me, but that's what happened. We hit a lick, not too far from here. Benny said he knew a place to fence what we took, so I left him to it. Problem was he never got back to me with my half. Took me a month to track him down. I had already decided that when I found him, I was gonna have to kill him. And that's what I did."

"You felt like you had to?" Lola asked.

"Yeah. That's the business. I'm sure you can see the parallels with what's happening now. Katrina, Rat, yeah, they're hoping to find what I took from them. But beyond that, they're looking to kill me for what I did. That's how this work goes. They'd be fools not to play by those rules."

Lola sucked in a deep breath through her nostrils. She watched him closely.

"The second one," Von continued, "is the only one I regret. I was a little older when it happened. A little wiser. I hit a million dollar home. Had good intel on the property, and I thought I did enough research on the homeowner. But me and my partner got interrupted on our way out. This lady, a rich broad. Old money. She walked through the front door with her driver. I didn't know he also served as her bodyguard. Me and my partner didn't have anywhere to hide, so we took up positions and waited for them to come our way.

"We planned to tie them up and bounce, but the driver was too gung ho. Took his job too seriously. We had the drop on them, but he reached for his shit. I shot him. My partner was about to take out the witness, but I made him stop. We tied the lady up and left, like we planned to, but that killing haunted me. To this day, I hate that it played out like that. The driver, he was just doing his job. Prolly had a wife and kids waiting for him to come home. He didn't deserve to die simply because I wanted to take that woman's valuables.

"It was that murder that made me start to look into nonlethal alternatives. That's when I started to carry a stun gun, like the one I used on Rat. And I started looking into tranquilizers. They don't work in the heat of the moment. If somebody got a gun on you, you don't wanna reach for something that'll take a few minutes to put them to sleep. But I've incapacitated a lot of people, when it would've been easier to kill them. I've done a lot of foul shit, but murder ain't never been something I take lightly."

He finished the rest of his bottle and placed it on the table. "The other two," he said, "they had it coming. I don't regret what happened to them at all. This was five years ago. I had a new crew that I put together. I was the mastermind. I researched every job we did, and I took care of selling what we got and dividing the pot.

"I had two brothers in the crew. They worked real good together. I didn't know that envy had begun to rear it's ugly head, but I should've seen it coming. Everyone in the crew knew I had more money than them. I had been in the game for much longer. They didn't need to see a list of my assets to know that I'd been handling my finances very well.

"These brothers, they tried to move on me. They were idiots. Both of 'em. They knew I took care of the security at every house we hit. If I can sit outside a property and disarm the security cameras with a laptop, what made them think the security at my house, *where I lay my head at night*, wasn't top notch? I saw them coming way before they broke into my house. I knew they planned to kill me before making off with whatever I had there, so I had no problem turning the tables on them. I put 'em both down, right there in the kitchen."

Lola saw that Von was looking at her but not really at her. She wondered if, in his mind's eye, he could see the scene clearly, like how she could still see her brother's murder with perfect clarity. If she followed her subconscious to that dark memory, she could even smell the blood.

"The gun I used had a silencer," Von said. "Later, I wondered if it would've been better if I used something different. If the neighbors had called the police and reported the gunshots, they would've came and got the bodies. It was three in the morning, so the killing would've been justifiable, on my part. But since the police didn't come, I had to learn how to clean up a murder scene and get rid of the bodies." He considered that and said, "I guess it was better that way. That was something I needed to learn how to do…"

He leaned forward and grabbed another small bottle of alcohol. He twisted the cap off and drank half of it, before returning his attention to her.

"Is that what you wanted to know?" he asked. "Is it what you expected?"

She sighed. She finished the bottle she'd been holding and placed it on the table.

"I don't know," she said honestly. "I don't know how I should feel."

He continued to watch her eyes before speaking. "You wanted to know if I'm some kind of monster," he prompted.

"Does hearing all of that settle the question for you, one way or another?"

"That's, um…" She swallowed. "I was hoping it would. But I still don't know. You said something about our moral compass. You're right. We're never gonna be aligned. Even if I can understand why you do what you do, I don't think I'll ever agree with it, or be okay with it."

He nodded. "I get that. I think, after what happened tonight, we're almost out of the woods. You should be able to go back to your normal life – if not tomorrow, then the day after. I would've taken you home tonight, but I'm still not sure it's safe."

"You don't think it's over?"

He shook his head. "Not the way things have gone. My crew, not counting Saul, there were four of us. I took care of two. That leaves one more. If Katrina came, I'm pretty sure Jugg is out there somewhere. He's gotta be in this city, waiting to make a move."

Lola felt the tendrils of fear return, inching down her body like serpents. She'd experienced so much tension today, the fear was not unexpected or uncomfortable.

"You said Jugg was the muscle?" she asked. "He's a big guy?"

"Built like a fucking truck," Von said. "That's how he got his name. You know that Marvel character Juggernaut?"

"No, I – I'm not into comics or Marvel movies."

"Well, you'll have to take my word for it. Jugg's a big dude. He'd break my neck if I ever tried to go head to head with him. But fortunately for us, all that brawn didn't come with brains. Without the tracker, I don't think Jugg has a clue what to do in this city – if he's even here."

"The tracker, you left it at the carnival?" She hadn't seen him retrieve it, but Von made a lot of moves she wasn't aware of.

"Yeah," he said, "it's still there. That means I have to look over my shoulder for a while longer. Tomorrow I'll head out again to see if the daylight brings more trouble."

Lola considered that. She didn't respond.

"I was surprised you wanted to go to the carnival with me tonight," he said. "You knew something might pop off."

"You said you wanted to take me out for our second date," she replied, smiling slightly.

"Yeah, and how'd that turn out for you? One minute we're on the Ferris wheel. Next thing you know, we got another body on our hands."

"I had fun tonight," she said. "Before the body."

He smiled and frowned at the same time. It was an interesting mix of expressions. "I know you think I'm the one who's mysterious, but you not that easy to figure out, either."

"I don't think the nature of our mystique is similar at all. I'm mysterious simply because I'm a woman. But you're mysterious on some Tom Cruise, Mission Impossible type of vibe."

He grinned at that and then asked, "Do you want me to book a separate room for you?"

Chuckling, she said, "You're asking me that *now*?"

"Well, yeah. I mean, after everything I told you, about the killing and stuff. I can understand if you don't feel comfortable around me."

Lola had considered this, even before Von told her about the people he killed. But now that the choice was hers, she shook her head. Maybe Von was right about her being hard to read.

She told him, "I don't want another room."

Von sensed she had made that decision based on fear and didn't question it. He finished his second drink and placed the empty bottle on the table.

"Don't look at me like that," he said. "There's barely a shot of alcohol in those things."

Laughing, she told him, "I didn't say anything. You feeling guilty about being an alcoholic?"

"Nah. I just don't wanna be judged for taking this one with me to the shower." He grabbed a third bottle before rising to his feet. "You have a shower in your bathroom too, or just a toilet?"

"Just a toilet. I used your shower yesterday, while you were out renting the car and whatever else you had going on."

"You know exactly what I was doing while I was gone. You wanna bathe first? I can wait."

"No, you go ahead." She pulled her phone from her back pocket. "I'm not in a rush. My friend's been texting me all day. I should respond to her."

Von took a few steps and then turned back and asked, "What are you gonna tell your friend, about where you are, what's been going on?"

"I'm gonna tell her I'm still with the man I went out with last night. Our first date was so amazing, we decided to spend a whole day together."

"One hell of a second date," he commented.

"The longest second date *ever*." She shook her head, smiling.

∞ ∞ ∞ ∞ ∞ ∞ ∞

Lola woke with a start. She sat up in bed, her heart thundering. It took a few moments for her to acclimate herself to the darkness. During that time, she reflected on what had awakened her. It was a nightmare. Rat and Katrina were both involved. But the more she thought about it, the harder it was for her to remember the specifics. She did, however, recall something that had troubled her during the dream.

Von had told her that he murdered his first soul because the man took off with the spoils from their burglary. Lola didn't agree with murder, in general, but that rationale made sense to her. As far as Jugg, wasn't he now in the same position? Von had taken off with the spoils from a job they did together. She could discount Saul and Rat, because they plotted against Von. But unless Von hadn't told her the whole story, Jugg was innocent. Katrina had been too. Von stole from them, and they deserved to come after him and get what was taken – or take his life if they couldn't retrieve the diamonds.

Lola caught herself and smiled weakly in the darkness.

Innocent?

The only innocent party in this sordid affair was the heir to the Campbell soup dynasty. All of the others, Von included, were horrible people.

So why was she leaving her bed to see if this horrible person was still awake? Lola checked the clock on the nightstand and saw that it was a quarter past one. She was aware that checking the time was only a formality. She would not have been deterred if it was a quarter past three.

Her footsteps were silent on the carpeted floor. She hesitated when she found the adjacent bedroom door closed.

She knocked softly, telling herself that if he didn't respond, that would be fate saving her from this prolonged tragedy. But Von responded immediately.

"What's up? I'm up. You can come in."

She opened the door cautiously, even though he had extended an invitation. The room was mostly dark, but he hadn't turned off the light in the bathroom. The illumination from that room allowed her to study his dark features as she walked into the room and took a seat on the side of his bed. Von first propped himself up on his elbows. He then scooted back to the headboard and sat up completely. Lola looked over her shoulder and met his eyes before speaking.

"I wanted to tell you that I understand why you had to do what you did to those people."

Von remained silent. He didn't know if she was talking about the murders or taking the diamonds from his last heist. He had never sought her approval, but her words made him feel a little better about the person he'd become.

"What are your plans, after this is all over?" she asked.

"I told you; I was hoping to come back here and settle down. Buy some property, give real estate a shot while I look into working with computers. There are a lot of houses in this city that could turn a nice profit if I invest in them. If everything goes well, I'll have enough money to make a serious go at it. I want to travel too. There are a lot of places I've always wanted to visit. I've never been out of the U.S...."

Lola nodded slightly. "You think it'll be safe for you to stay here, in Overbrook Meadows, after all that's happened?"

Von had been wondering the same thing. "Probably not – not until Jugg and Saul are out of the picture."

Out of the picture. A not so veiled way to say *dead.* More murders.

Lola looked away from him, until she was facing the open door she'd entered through. She wasn't typically the shy type, but she needed to break eye contact before asking, "What about me?"

Watching her back, the question caught Von off guard. "What do you mean? I know you want to go home. I'm doing everything I can to make that happen, to make sure it's safe for you there."

"No, I mean if you stay in this city. Do I fit into your plan, once everything is over?"

That comment was even more surprising. Von considered his response before saying, "I didn't think you'd want to have anything to do with me when this is over. I know I hurt you. I put you in a position you didn't deserve to be in. I thought you'd want to go back to your old life as soon as possible."

Lola took a deep breath. She was equally confused, by her own thoughts. Von had upended her normal, *boring* but safe lifestyle. Getting as far away from him as possible was the only sensible outcome. For the life of her, she could not understand why that wasn't what she wanted.

She felt movement on the bed behind her. She didn't look back. A moment later, Von moved into a seated position beside her. She turned to look at him. He found her expression unreadable. Her pupils swam in a pool of fear and uncertainty. But fear wasn't her overriding emotion. Von didn't think so. He reached for her hands, which she was cradling in her lap. He saw that beyond her tee shirt, her legs were bare. The tee shirt was just long enough to conceal her panties while she was seated. He wondered if she was wearing panties at all.

He took one of her hands in his and leaned closer. He hesitated for only a moment, allowing her time to rebuff his advance. When she remained still, he kissed her, softly. Her fingers wrapped around his hand, squeezing slightly. He deepened the kiss, first licking and then sucking her bottom lip. She returned the affection. Von's free hand moved around her back and settled on her side. He caressed the space between her breast and love handle. His blood rushed, hot and eager.

He was embarrassed by how quickly his body responded to her. He didn't think Lola noticed. She couldn't have. Her eyes were closed as they continued kissing. But she released his hand, and her fingers made their way between his legs. She sucked air around his tongue when she felt how hard he was. Without pretense, her hand slipped beneath the waistband of his boxers so she could feel him, all of him.

Von was struck by a strong sense of déjà vu. It had been approximately 24 hours since they were in this same position. They were in a different hotel, and on the sofa instead of the bed, but everything about this moment was delightfully familiar. Von remembered how she had taken him into her mouth that night, how surprised he was, how good her tongue and lips felt on his manhood. He had fought hard against cumming in her mouth, but he wasn't able to suppress his pre-cum. He knew Lola had tasted it, because she sucked him harder as she swallowed it down.

His hand slipped deeper into her lap. He thought she might have spread her legs for him. When his anxious fingers discovered that she was not, in fact, wearing panties, she spread her legs even wider. He was sure of it this time. He didn't have to slip any fingers inside her oasis to know how wet she was, but he did it anyway. She pulled her lips away and gasped. Her right hand moved to the mattress to brace herself as she leaned back on the bed. Her other hand was still in his boxers, stroking him now.

Unexpectedly, Von slipped off the bed and positioned himself on his knees, his head squarely between her legs. He lifted her thighs and pushed her further back onto the mattress. Lola's eyes were half closed, drunken with longing. She used her arms to scoot back, until she was in the position he wanted her in. She watched him first stare at her box and then dive in face first. She reclined fully then. The immediate surge of pleasure as his lips wrapped around her clitoris sent a warm numbness down her legs.

Oh. Oh...

Her mouth fell open. Her eyes slipped closed. One hand moved between her legs. She first touched his head tentatively before palming and rubbing his hair, encouraging him as he lapped up her juices. He seamlessly transitioned between sucking her clit, then licking it, and then sucking it again. She lost track of time and did not fight the blinding pink sensations that rolled down her frame and converged on her box. Her orgasm was all encompassing. She wasn't aware that her ass slid across the sheets and then left the bed in spurts as she bucked against his face, urging him to suck harder and lick deeper.

Von responded like her pussy was a papaya, and he hadn't eaten in days. He didn't stop until her orgasms began to roll in waves. Back to back. Each one zapping more and more of her strength and sanity. She was only vaguely aware that at some point he withdrew his lips and wonderful tongue. She thought she heard him walk across the room, but with the blood rushing past her ears; she might have imagined it.

One thing she did not imagine was his return. Condom in place, dick rock hard, Von mounted her in the missionary position. Lola thought she was completely spent, but her body reacted to him. She spread her legs wider and raised her knees as he plunged deep inside her.

Another flash of lightning erupted behind her closed eyelids. So beautifully vibrant their lovemaking was, like a bag full of diamonds.

CHAPTER TEN
TOO EASY

Making me fall for you – why?
You're not an honest, stand-up guy
I see the cunning in your eyes
The dark deception, not trying to hide
I could've been in my own bed tonight
Instead I'm riding this forbidden high
What happens to me when you decide
That I've never been the type
Of woman you needed in your life?

The next morning, they ordered room service, rather than head downstairs to the hotel's restaurant. Von was fairly sure they wouldn't have a repeat of their breakfast twenty-four hours ago, but *fairly sure* wasn't one hundred percent sure.

Twenty-four hours.

It was hard to believe the first encounter with Rat occurred so recently. Von felt like everything that transpired since he spotted Rat at breakfast happened over a week, or at least a few days' time. The strides he'd made with Lola, their ups and downs, the smiles, tears, and glorious lovemaking...

They'd experienced more drama in one day than most couples experience for the duration of their relationship. Not that he and Lola were a couple. As much as he liked her, he wasn't foolish enough to think that her feelings for him were more than grief shrouded with self-preservation. Once she was safe to return to her normal life, he suspected she would run as far away from him as she could.

"What are we doing today?" she asked as she cut into the French toast she'd ordered. She also had two eggs and a couple of slices of bacon on the side. The smell of freshly brewed coffee saturated the hotel room.

Von had opted for an omelet with sausage. Looking at Lola's meal, he wished he'd ordered the same as her.

"I'm gonna test the waters," he said, "see if I can draw out Jugg. If not him, maybe another one of Saul's goons is looking for me."

Lola's mouth watered when the food was delivered, but that news made her stomach turn. She began to pick at her meal, rather than wolf it down like she planned to.

She asked him, "How you gonna do that?"

"Only way I can think of is drive around, see who's following me. I'll start by going to the carnival. Might not have any luck there. Yesterday was their last night. I'm sure they're breaking it down today, shipping the rides to the next city or state. I'm gonna try to get in there and grab the tracker, if I can find it."

"You think they're breaking the carnival down already?"

"Yeah, I've seen it happen. Everything you saw last night can fit into a dozen eighteen wheelers. Every day they leave it there is costing them money they could be making at a different location."

"You think you can get in while they're doing that – breaking it down?"

"I've gotten into much more secure places."

Lola took a sip of her coffee. It was really good. She drank a little more and then sighed.

"You don't think that's dangerous?" she asked. "Getting the tracker and having it on you?"

He nodded. Judging by the way he continued eating casually, he didn't share her apprehension.

"It's risky," he acknowledged. "But I can't think of another way to make them show themselves. It worked with Rat – Katrina too. After I get the tracker, I'll take it to some random spots, wait for them to show up, and figure out what I gotta do to deal with them. If no one shows after today, I'll feel more confident about sending you home and selling the diamonds."

"What about Saul?" she asked. "You said Rat probably told him where you are."

"I may have to pay him a visit," Von agreed. "I'm taking this one step at a time. Any threats that might be waiting on me outside this hotel are my immediate concern. I'll deal with the ones in California later."

Lola took a deep breath. She hoped the stress would leave her with the exhalation, but it didn't.

She asked him, "Do you want me to go with you?"

Frowning, he said, "Why would you want to do that?"

She shrugged. "I don't want to be here alone. Plus, we're in this together, right?"

That was the second time she spoke those words. The first time she mentioned it, Von gave in, but this time he asked, "What does that mean to you – that we're in this together?"

She didn't expect the question. He could see it in her eyes.

"You said they were after both of us."

"Yes, but they're only after you as a means to get to me. That doesn't mean I should expose you to danger. You don't have a stake in this game. I have to keep you out of trouble and keep myself alive. None of that is your responsibility."

"Yeah, but I don't want you to leave me here alone while you're putting yourself in danger. What if they come for you, and it's more of them than you can handle by yourself? I can give you another set of eyes. Maybe I'll see something that you don't."

Von stopped eating. He put his fork down and said, "That's a possibility. But you should think about what you just said. If I run into trouble that's more than I can handle, do you think you could do anything to stop it? If anything, they'll kill both of us, instead of just me. I think it's better if you stay here, safe, while I deal with this problem that I created."

"And if something happens to you, what am I supposed to do?" she wondered.

"If something happens to me, then they got what they wanted. You can go home. Back to your nine-to-five. Your regular life."

Lola knew how ridiculous it would sound if she told him she didn't want that life anymore, so she kept the comment to herself.

Instead she asked, "How will I know if you're in trouble?"

Grimly, he told her, "If I don't come back, and I'm not responding to your calls, that will be your answer."

She couldn't hide her frustration with his line of thinking. "It's that easy for you, to just go and maybe never come back, while I'm sitting here worried about you the whole time?"

His eyes softened. "I didn't say it would be easy. I'll be on the lookout from the moment I leave this hotel. The stress, combined with my feelings for you, hoping I'll come back to you... It won't be easy for me. But it'll be worse if I take you with me and something happens to you. I couldn't live with myself if something like that happened. If I die, it'll be because I deserve it. You don't."

Lola suddenly felt foolish about her line of thinking. Von planned to expose himself to enemies who meant him harm. If they killed him, it would be tragic, but by his own admission, he deserved to die for what he did to these people.

That's the business. They'd be fools not to play by those rules.

She asked him, "Will you at least respond if I text you, to let me know you're alright?"

He nodded. "I will." After a few beats, he said, "You should eat. Your food looks really good."

"I'm not hungry," she admitted. "Maybe I'll reheat it and have it for lunch."

"Fuck that. Order something else for lunch. Matter-of-fact, I want you to order the most expensive thing on the menu for lunch. You deserve it."

"Why?" she asked, grinning, "because of the way I sucked your dick on our first date?"

Stunned, it took him a moment to formulate a response. "No, because of the way I ate your pussy last night."

"You rewarding me for eating my pussy? Don't you think it should be the other way around."

"Nope." He shook his head, returning to his meal. "Last night, the pleasure was all mine."

∞ ∞ ∞ ∞ ∞ ∞ ∞

Von locked in and became wary the moment he left the hotel room. This was an endeavor he considered himself well versed in. He'd been honing these skills since his first burglary. He was solo back then, a few years out of high school, barely old enough to grow a moustache. On that day, he'd left an unoccupied residence in the dead of night, lugging a blanket full of goodies over his back. He hadn't been prepared for what he might find in the home, and once inside, he was equally unprepared for how he would transport the stolen goods to his getaway car, which was parked down the street.

Always adaptable, he began tossing valuables onto the bed in the master bedroom. When he had collected all he could in the short time he allowed himself in the residence, he pulled the four corners of the blanket into a large bindle and made his escape, looking like the very opposite of Santa Claus – skinny, black, taking, rather than giving. As he made his way down the darkened street, he looked around feverishly, while still trying to appear casual. He checked the neighbors' houses, to see if anyone was on their porch in the wee hours of the night or if the shades were parted in any of the windows, and a nosey face was peering out at him.

When he made it to his car that night, sweating, his heart pounding, he felt better about his chances now that he was no longer exposed. But he continued to check his surroundings as he made his getaway. No one from the neighborhood watch followed him out of the area, and no police car swooped in behind him before he made it to his hideout.

Since then, Von had honed his reconnaissance skills to near perfection. He scouted every potential target for days, sometimes weeks, to ensure the success of his crew. He put these same skills to work when they made their getaway. The fact that he'd never been arrested after decades in the business spoke volumes about how carefully proficient he was.

In the hallway of his hotel, at ten o'clock in the morning, he encountered two guests and two housekeepers. None of these faces were familiar, but Von did not take solace in that. If Saul had sent goons, they could be anywhere and anyone. Von walked to the elevator but didn't press the down button right away. He waited. After thirty seconds, he stepped back into the hallway and looked right and then left. One of the housekeepers had slipped inside a room to prepare it for the next guest. The other housekeeper approached a door and knocked.

She announced herself, "*Housekeeping*," before using a keycard to gain entry into the room. A moment later, she was out of sight as well.

The two guests he'd encountered had also disappeared, presumably back inside their hotel room. Von pressed the button on the elevator. A minute passed before the doors opened for him. No stranger appeared at the last minute to follow him down to the lobby. He stepped into the elevator alone.

In the lobby, there were plenty of faces to scan. Von did so quickly as he walked. He did not see anyone he recognized. He certainly didn't see Jugg's hulking figure sipping coffee in the hotel's restaurant. This made him feel a little better, but he didn't exhale a sigh of relief until he made it to the parking lot and got into his rental. Once there, he waited again. He started the car and sat idling for a full five minutes. A few guests exited the hotel, but none looked suspicious. No one looked around, looked for him, as they emerged from the automatic doors rolling suitcases behind them.

Von put the car in gear and drove out of the parking lot, scanning the area for threats as he did so.

On the streets, he did his usual tricks to see if he had a tail. Four consecutive right turns put him back on the same road. He was positive none of the cars behind him had made the same turns, but he tried again, with left turns this time. Still no takers. He then took his possible followers to a parking garage. It took him fifteen minutes to find the right one. It was six stories high. He drove up ramp after ramp before backing into a spot on the fourth floor. He waited there for another ten minutes. Still nothing.

Finally confident that he was not being pursued, Von left the parking garage and drove straight to Fossil Creek.

∞ ∞ ∞ ∞ ∞ ∞ ∞

The carnival site looked a lot different in the daylight hours. As he entered the property, Von saw that some of the attractions had already been dismantled.

They didn't waste any time, he told himself. But this was perfect.

There were no longer any event security guards patrolling the site. Even better, there were no police officers.

Instead, the area was crawling with carnies, contractors and laborers. As predicted, a dozen eighteen wheelers had converged in the parking lot. Twelve hours ago, this lot was filled with civilian vehicles. Now, it was big rigs and dusty pickup trucks.

Von parked next to one of the pickups, as if he had every right to be there, and exited his vehicle. He casually walked to the back of the rental and opened the lift gate. He had a duffle bag in the trunk, but he wasn't fully prepared for this venture. If so, he would've brought a hardhat with him. The only thing he had that might prove helpful was the safety vest he'd donned when he walked down the alley behind Lola's house with a weed eater in hand.

He put the vest on, closed the lift gate, and walked to the entrance of the carnival, which would be nothing more than a vacant lot by days' end. Two days tops. He encountered half a dozen curious looks as he ventured deeper into the carnival grounds, but none of the laborers questioned him. He encountered resistance for the first time from a man dressed in jeans, work boots, and a golf shirt that was tucked in neatly. This was the first person Von had seen who remained clean and had no sweat on his brow.

"Hey," the man said, walking directly to him. His eyes narrowed as he looked Von up and down. "Who you working for? I don't recognize you..."

"I'm from the city," Von said. "Came to check on how things are going. I know you guys are professionals, but... You know how it is."

The man nodded, smiling slightly. "Fossil Creek, they already sent somebody." His voice had a southern twang that reminded Von more of Mississippi than Texas. "That guy, he was here bright and early, said he'd be back later."

Von played the trump card without missing a beat. "I'm with Overbrook Meadows, not Fossil Creek. I won't be here long. Promise not to get in your way."

The man nodded. His smile slipped a little. Von knew that look well. This man was in charge and felt that he was fully capable of dismantling a carnival without oversight.

"That's fine," the man said. "Do what you gotta do. Stay as long as you want. But I run a tight ship. You're not gonna find anything out of order. Most of the Mexicans don't speak English, but they're all here legally, if that's what you're looking for."

"I don't give a shit about that," Von said. "Long as nobody dies and you don't leave a bunch of holes in the ground when you're done, we got no problems. I don't even care if your workers have a beer with lunch, as long as nobody gets seriously hurt."

The contractor's smile returned, full flair this time.

He said, "I can assure you none of that is gonna happen – not even the beers at lunch. You didn't bring a hardhat? I got one I can give you."

"I won't be here long enough to need one, but if it'll make you feel better if I wear it, I don't mind."

"If you're gonna be hanging out where they're taking the rides down, I'd feel better if you have it. Last thing I need is someone from the city getting injured."

"I'm not going that far," Von told him. "Just need to be here long enough to say I was here, and I met the man in charge. Speaking of which, if that's you, I need your name."

"Travis Daniels," the contractor said.

He offered a hand. As Von shook it, he noticed it was strong and calloused.

"Nice to meet you, Mr. Daniels."

"Likewise. And you are...?"

"Lewis Willoughby. I'll be gone in five, ten minutes tops."

Daniels continued to smile as he shook his hand. Clearly, that was music to his ears.

∞ ∞ ∞ ∞ ∞ ∞ ∞

After their introduction, Daniels left him alone, and Von wandered directly to the carnival games. Most of the laborers were busy on the other side of the park. Von was curious about how they'd take down the Ferris wheel he and Lola had been on the night before, but not curious enough to head to that operation or stick around afterwards to watch it come down. In the game area, the attendants who had begged passersby for money last night were replaced with laborers, mostly men, all Hispanic. They shot glances at Von as he approached the area, but they had seen him speaking to their boss a moment ago. If Daniels had given Von the okay to be there, it wasn't their responsibility to investigate further. They assumed Von was there to check on their work, so they kicked their operation up another notch.

The workers in this area were skilled. Rather than damage any of the wooden booths or contraptions, they used the claw end of their hammers to remove nails, hoping to maintain the integrity of the material for future use. The area was barely recognizable, but Von found the water gun attraction and began to snoop around the area, doubtful that he would find the tracker in the shell that remained of what had been a brightly lit game.

Von nodded as a form of greeting as he drew closer to the workers. They nodded back. None questioned him as he stepped deeper into their workspace and began to scan the ground for the tracker. He felt this was an impossible mission. The debris, coupled with the scrutiny, along with the fact that the tracker was the size of a half dollar and roughly the same color as the earth it lie on, made him doubtful of his chances.

But sometimes, luck is on your side.

He bent and retrieved something that was slightly glistening in the morning sunlight.

It was the tracker.

He slipped it into his pocket, while the workers watched him.

As he walked away from the area, he encountered the head contractor again. Mr. Daniels had a spare hard hat in hand.

"Here you go," he said, offering it to Von. "Don't want any OSHA folks coming down on me for allowing you back here without protection."

"Actually, I was just leaving," Von said. "Told you I was only here to check a box."

The contractor smiled. "Well, alrighty, Mr. Willoughby. You have a nice day."

∞ ∞ ∞ ∞ ∞ ∞ ∞

He called Lola when he got back on the road.

"What's up. How you holding up?"

"I should be asking you that," she breathed. "Where are you? What happened?"

He told her what he'd been up to.

"Where are you going now?" she asked when he was done speaking.

"Gonna drive around for a while, see if I got any takers. I'ma stop for lunch, maybe hit up one of the malls. Leave the tracker in the food court and wait there. If anyone's tracking it, they should come running, once they see it's on the move again."

"You don't seem to think any of this is dangerous..."

"No, I understand what I'm getting myself into. On the road especially. But once I get to the mall, I doubt if they'd try anything in a crowded location. They won't know I'm watching and waiting to see them before they see me."

"What happens if they come for the tracker at the mall?"

"Haven't decided yet."

That didn't sound like the master planner she'd come to know. "What if no one comes for you at the mall? Is that it? Is it over?"

"Yeah, I think so," he said. "I'm gonna leave the tracker at the mall, and then I'll head back to one of my houses where I left the Tahoe. I'll be ready to sell the diamonds, but first I gotta get rid of that SUV. I don't see any way the police could fuck around and find it, but if they did, I'd be headed to the pen for sure."

She surprised him by asking, "Can you come get me, before you go to that house?"

In the time he hesitated to respond, she knew what he was thinking.

She said, "You need someone to help you with the Tahoe, don't you? I can drive the rental and follow you to wherever you plan to get rid of it. Don't you think that's a good idea?"

Actually, Von thought that was an excellent idea, but not with her involvement. His plan was to find a place to torch the Tahoe. He should probably wait till nightfall, but if he could pull it off during the daytime, he would. Considering the attention the smoke would draw, a speedy getaway was crucial.

"I don't know," he told her.

"Von, we're in this together."

He knew she didn't understand the full implications of that statement. Even still, those words had a calming effect that she probably wasn't aware of.

"Besides," she continued, "the longer I'm here by myself, the more worried and scared I am. When I'm with you, I don't have to worry."

Von started to tell her about the multiple times he'd seen her so worried that her fair skin had taken on an ashen paleness – *while she was with him* – but he refrained.

He said, "Even if I don't have the tracker with me when I make it back to you, that doesn't mean we're in the clear."

"I know. I still wanna go."

At that precise moment, Von realized he was falling in love with her. Some would say that was ludicrous. He'd known her for less than a week. Love at first sight was a foolish man's delusion. But at this stage of his life, he was too old to argue with his emotions.

"Alright," he decided. "I'll come get you. But it'll be a few hours before I get back."

She told him, "That's alright."

"Okay. I'll call you later."

He fought against a nonsensical urge to tack on, *I love you*, before he ended the call.

He wondered if she had fought the same urge before telling him, "Alright. Please be careful."

Frowning at his own uncertainty, Von told her, "Okay, I will," and disconnected.

151

CHAPTER ELEVEN
THINGS THAT GO BUMP
IN THE NIGHT

Booming firearms like cannons
Shakes the life from foes. Abandoned
Bodies free of souls – transfixed
With burning, gaping holes betwixt
Their eyes: Mowed down for small infractions
Big badass sat down for actin
Tougher than the ones with pistols
The Cha-Chick of guns cocked is crystal
Clear to hoodlums in the know
Split-seconds count – head for the flo'
Chin-check the do', lest medics find
Yo big bad ass stuck out of time

Von returned to the hotel room a little after three p.m. Despite the erotic lovemaking they'd experienced the night before, he was surprised when Lola rose to her feet and wrapped her arms around him as he stepped through the doorway. He kicked the door closed with his foot and returned the affection. He questioned the sentiments that flooded his senses as he buried his face against the side of her neck. The warmth of her body shouldn't feel this good.

She released him and backed away, smiling broadly.

"I'm glad you're back."

"Me too," he uttered.

"I take it no one came after you," she said. "You got rid of the tracker?"

Von filled her in on the past few hours. After leaving the carnival site, he made his way to an Applebee's restaurant, watching his six the whole time. Inside the restaurant, he made sure to be seated with his eyes on the entrance. The tracker in his front pocket felt like a lead weight. And his nerves were so bad, the food wasn't appetizing at all. But he took his time with the meal and left the restaurant an hour later.

His next stop was Hulen Mall. He went first to the food court and slipped the tracker beneath one of the metal garbage bins. He found a seat a safe distance away and pretended to peruse his cellphone as he watched the shoppers. No one came to the area and inspected the trach can. He left the food court and texted Lola, asking for her size. She asked why before providing the information. Knowing she hadn't brought many clothes with her, he found a Gap store and bought a few outfits that were attractive to him and hopefully pleasing to her.

He then returned to the food court and took the seat he'd occupied earlier. He watched the area for another hour before walking to the trash bin and bending to tie his shoe. He collected the tracker and left the mall.

Still no one.

After driving for another thirty minutes, Von was finally convinced that no one was keeping up with him by way of the tracker. He tossed it out of the window on I-30 and headed for the woman who had been waiting for him.

"I hope that means it's all over," Lola said, her eyes twinkling.

Von thought about Saul, who was usually reserved and softspoken. He had murdered most of Saul's crew, but Saul had the means to establish another one. He also had a group of armed men at his disposal at any time.

He couldn't force these thoughts from his mind, but he nodded.

"Yeah. I think we're good. If they're not using the tracker to find me, they don't have any other way."

"That's good. Are you ready to go get the Tahoe?"

"Not now," he told her. "The more I think about it, the more I feel like that's not something I wanna do while it's still light outside."

"Okay. That makes sense." She took a seat on the sofa and crossed her legs as she leaned back into the cushions. "What do you wanna do until then?"

She probably didn't mean that to be an erotic invitation, but there was something in her eyes, an allure that she probably wasn't aware of, that sparked burning embers in Von's chest.

"I know it's a little late for lunch," he said, "but if you're hungry, we could–"

She shook her head. "We can get dinner later. I ended up eating all of my breakfast while you were gone. I'm not hungry."

"Yeah, me neither," he said. "How about we–"

"How about you sit down and stop trying to entertain me. You been ripping and running all day. Come here. Take a break."

Von didn't feel tired, but he welcomed the opportunity to be closer to her. He took a seat on the sofa, bringing his shopping bag into his lap.

"Is that for me?" she asked, her eyes dancing.

Von didn't feel self-conscious when he went to the department store, but looking down at the bags from the Gap, he told her, "Sorry. It wasn't a real shopping trip. Next time, you should go with me. We can hit up some better stores."

"Why you say that? I like the Gap. You think I'm bougie?"

Smiling, he shook his head. "No, I don't think that."

"Let me see what you got."

He handed over the bags, and she sorted through the items inside. Jeans, underwear, and tee shirts. Lola was surprised by an item at the bottom of the second bag. She pulled it out and eyed him curiously.

"I thought it smelled good," Von said, looking at the perfume. "We're not going anywhere special, but I thought you'd like to wear it one day."

Her smile was the best outcome he could've hoped for.

"You found this at the Gap?"

"No. There was a Macy's in the mall. I probably should've got your clothes from there."

"I told you I'm cool with the Gap." She used her nails to tear through the plastic on the perfume. "Stop trying to make me out to be some gold-digger."

"Sorry. I didn't mean to."

She got the box open and pulled the perfume free of it. She spritzed a little on her wrist, gave it a whiff, and then spritzed once more on her neck.

"Come here," she said, pulling him closer. "Tell me what you think. I heard that perfume smells different on each person because of the way the chemicals react to the chemicals in our body."

"I never heard that." He leaned closer, first sniffing her neck and then fully inhaling the divine chemistry she'd created.

"See. I told you."

She leaned to the side, so that her legs were fully outstretched on the sofa. Von followed her into the reclined position, resting his head on her chest. She reached over him and rubbed his back with one hand. The other hand caressed the side of his head. Von closed his eyes. He felt so good in the embrace, he didn't realize she was putting him to sleep until coherent thoughts escaped him and his breaths became shallow with slumber.

∞ ∞ ∞ ∞ ∞ ∞ ∞

He awakened several hours later. He sat up and looked up at Lola, who had also fallen asleep. She looked so peaceful, so beautiful, he considered leaving her behind for his next mission. But she stirred when he pushed off the sofa and rose to his feet. Her drowsy eyes moved from him to the window on the far side of the room. The fire in the sky had gone away. Overbrook Meadows was enveloped in darkness.

Sitting up, she asked him, "You ready?"

He nodded. "I brought you a dark outfit. Black top and bottom. You need to put that on."

"Okay."

She stood and made her way to her bedroom. Von watched her walk away before heading to his own room.

Twenty minutes later, they were on the road again. They didn't speak much as Von drove. He wasn't as apprehensive as he'd been earlier that day, when the threat of someone pursuing him felt like a strong possibility. But with Lola with him, he remained attentive. He didn't spot any tails as they made their way to his second property on the west side of town. He looked around warily as he pulled into the driveway. The porch light was on, as it always was. From the rental car, he could see the work boots he'd left on the porch as a decoy.

He wasn't sure about the validity of the deterrent, but he'd heard that intruders, particularly those who prey on single women, are less likely to target a home if they believe a man lived there. He'd purchased this property six months ago and never spent the night there. Between the work boots and the porch light, something had deterred the city's night walkers from breaking into this home. These security features were even more important tonight, because in addition to the Tahoe he had to get rid of, his diamonds were stashed in this house. He wondered how Lola would react when she finally laid her eyes on them.

Would she think that everything they'd been through had been worth it? He doubted it, but it may make it easier for her to understand his motivation, why he had to drag her into this unreal saga.

He used an app on his phone to activate the garage door. As it rose, the garage light came on, and his Tahoe came into view. The wheels of the SUV were caked with mud from their trip to the duck pond. Dried mud also stained the side of the vehicle. Von felt an ominous sense of dread as he pulled into the two car garage. He looked over at Lola. Her eyes were wide and unblinking. He guessed the sight of the Tahoe had the same effect on her.

He killed the engine on the Infiniti and lowered the garage door. The moment he stepped out of the rental, he wished he'd left the garage door open. Although the Tahoe had only been parked there for one day, it was warm outside, and the air in the garage was almost stifling. The scent of mud, gasoline, and decomposition hit him like a slap to the face. Despite knowing full well that Rat's body was no longer in the vehicle, Von wouldn't have been surprised to find the dead man folded up in the back – the stench was that bad.

As he walked further into the garage and made his way to the back of the Tahoe, he saw dried blood smeared on the bumper, from when he had dragged Rat's body out of the vehicle. He didn't remember seeing that before. He marveled at the sight, thinking of all the places he'd driven after they left Rat's body in Forest Hill. The blood stood out flagrantly against the Tahoe's white paint. It was unlike him to be so careless. If he'd been pulled over by an eagle-eyed policeman, everything he'd done would've unraveled.

He looked back at Lola, who was slowly following him through the garage. She couldn't hide the look of disdain the smells and sight of the Tahoe brought her. He wouldn't have been surprised if she dug in her heels and told him, *Nope. Can't do it. Take me back to the hotel.* But she kept walking. A moment later, Von opened the garage door and led her into the house, which looked and smelled a lot differently.

He flipped the light on in the kitchen, revealing a modern design with granite countertops and sleek, new appliances. The expression Lola had worn in the garage was replaced with relief and fascination. She'd expected this place to look similar to the first house he took her to, where the contractors still had a ton of work to do, and the smell of paint and sheetrock filled every room. By contrast, this house was beautiful, ready for a family or a bachelor to move right in. From the kitchen, she saw that the living room was unfurnished, but that only added to the allure, making the place seem more spacious.

"You own this house?" she asked him.

"Yeah. I plan to rent it out. Gonna hire a property manager to take care of this one and the other one, once it's ready to go."

"How come you don't want to live here?" she wondered. "This place is beautiful. A lot better than my house."

"I never planned to live here," he explained. "I told you I was looking into some business ventures, for when this is all over."

Noticing he was still walking, moving deeper into the house, she asked him, "Where you going?"

"I need to grab something before we head out. You can wait here. I'll be back in a second."

He disappeared down one of the hallways. Lola watched the empty hallway for a second before turning back to admire the kitchen. The stove, dishwasher and fridge were all stainless steel. She pulled open one of the cabinets and found it empty, in pristine condition. She noticed a Phillips screwdriver on the countertop. She guessed it had been left by the workers who installed the new cabinets.

She heard a sound, a loud BOOMP! followed by an even louder noise. Her heart shot up in her throat as her attention snapped back to the hallway where she'd last seen Von. Her first thought was that he'd fallen. But the BOOMP!

was followed by more sounds. Thrashing. Grunting. Something was bumping against the wall, not far from her.

Was he having a seizure?

That didn't seem likely, but she had to remind herself that she didn't really know this man. Von may very well have a medical ailment that he had not disclosed. She sprinted in the direction of the noise, her heart knocking against her sternum. She expected to find any number of things in the hallway, but none of it prepared her for the sight that awaited her.

She was so stunned, she froze in place, her eyes wide, her jaw dropping by degrees. Several crucial, life-saving moments passed as she wrapped her mind around the fact that Von was not alone in the hallway. He'd been ambushed. The interloper, a bald, white man with a full beard, was nearly twice Von's size. He'd already taken full advantage of his considerable girth and easily overpowered his opponent. Von was taller than Lola, and she'd admired his slender, muscular frame. But compared to the other man, Von was rendered virtually defenseless. As she watched, the bigger man swung him around like a rag doll as he fought to secure a rear naked choke.

Jugg.

The name flashed in her mind like fireworks.

This realization was followed by a multitude of questions, but none of those answers would alter what she was witnessing.

Both men hit the floor with another hard crash that seemed to rock the whole house. Von grimaced, his teeth bared. He fought valiantly to avoid the inevitable, but it was no use. Jugg had both arms wrapped tightly around him. Von thrashed out with his legs and fists. He kicked the walls so hard he left dents in the sheetrock. He threw a flurry of punches over his shoulder that landed solidly on Jugg's face, but the big man showed no reaction, even as blood spilled from his nose. Despite Von's efforts to thwart the attack, Jugg expertly twisted his writhing body into the position he wanted. With Von's back pressed against his chest, Jugg began to work his right arm under his chin.

Von gripped the offensive arm with both hands, fighting with all that he had in him to keep the crook of Jugg's arm away from his throat, but he was unsuccessful. Jugg's arms were the size of thick tree branches. His neck and chest were equally formidable. As she watched, still in a state of semi-paralysis, Lola realized that all of the sounds she heard came from Von. He grunted, panted, and knocked the walls with his failing legs. Jugg, on the other hand, had not made a sound. He was calm, sure, and efficient.

The larger man lie flat on his back with Von struggling on top of him. He wrapped both of his massive legs around Von's lower body and was able to secure the chokehold with minimal effort. Lola finally broke free of her immobility when she saw Von's eyes grow as large as silver dollars. Even with his brown skin, she saw the blood rush from his face as his air supply was partially cut off. Von tried to tuck his chin to prevent the chokehold from becoming more secure, but he could not stop or even slow the inevitable. Jugg went in for the kill by rolling both of their bodies. They remained in the same position, with Jugg choking him from behind, but now Jugg was fully on top of him. His weight made it even more unlikely that Von would be able to draw a breath into his lungs or free himself from this seasoned killer.

Lola considered her options and quickly deduced that they were limited. She'd seen Von punch this man in the face with all he had. Jugg's nose was bleeding so badly, it might have been broken, but he hadn't been deterred in the slightest. Lola turned and raced back to the kitchen. She returned seconds later with the only weapon at her disposal. Without hesitating, she lunged forward and stabbed Jugg in the back with the screwdriver. The first blow hit nothing but muscle. Even though the shaft of the tool was almost fully submerged in the rippling flesh, Jugg registered no reaction.

Her eyes filled with tears, her hands trembling, Lola yanked the tool out of the wound and tried again. This time she used both hands as she slammed it down dead center in his back. The shaft didn't go down nearly as much this time before its forward momentum was impeded by hard bone. Jugg emitted a surprised sound that was somewhere between a cough and a grunt. His arm left Von's throat, and a meaty hand reached back to the source of the pain. Given his bulk, Lola didn't think he'd have the flexibility to make contact with the screwdriver, but he did. Through horror-filled eyes, she watched as he pawed at the handle of the tool.

It struck her that there was no blood coming from this wound. She was also acutely aware that if he managed to rip the screwdriver free, he would no doubt use it to finish off Von.

And then he'd turn his sights on her.

Her next move came with no cunning or foresight. Even as she moved, it didn't feel like it was her who was doing it. She felt as though she was merely a passenger in her own body as she charged forward again. Her eyes were panicked, but her teeth were clenched, and the animalistic sound that escaped her lips was reminiscent of ancestors she had never known, though they'd always lived within her and empowered her with the most basic instinct to protect what was hers.

She stomped the handle of the screwdriver with all the strength her calves and thigh muscles could muster. She didn't initially feel the pain of the rounded handle slamming into the bottom of her sneaker, but Jugg's reaction was immediate, although not at all what she'd expected.

He simply stopped.

Everything.

His arms fell to his sides. His legs became still. His whole body went completely limp. Standing over him, panting, adrenaline rushing through her bloodstream with the speed of a bullet, Lola saw that she'd driven the screwdriver deep inside him, all the way to the handle. There still wasn't any blood seeping from the wound, but there was no doubt that the damage had been done. She thought she hit bone the first time she stabbed him there. Her foot had finished the job, driving the metal through his spine.

She stood, panting, waiting. She heard breathing coming from the pile of bodies at her feet. One of the sounds was deep and guttural. She thought Jugg was dead, but as she watched, she was able to attribute this sound to him. She could see his torso rise and fall with each shuddering breath. Beneath him, she thought she heard more breathing. She prayed that this was Von but didn't allow hope to settle into her psyche until she heard him speak.

"*Lola.*" His voice was painfully raspy. "*Are, are you okay?*"

His breathing was labored. Lola couldn't find her voice to respond.

"*Hel, help me,*" he pleaded. "*Get him off me. I – I can't breathe.*"

The tears that had been threatening to spill for the past few minutes came with the torrents of a thunderstorm.

"Baby, I'm here," she cried. She knelt next to the bodies and gripped Jugg's shoulder with both hands. She pulled with all her might but was unable to make any headway. *"I can't. I can't move him."*

"I'ma help," Von breathed. *"We'll try together."*

"Okay, baby. I'm ready."

Even with both of them exerting maximum effort, they were unable to roll Jugg onto his side. After several failed attempts, Von resorted to crawling from beneath the downed man. Three minutes after Lola stomped the screwdriver into the juggernaut's spine, Von was finally free.

CHAPTER TWELVE
FIFTEEN MILLION REASONS WHY

Jugg had been in town the whole time. That was the only explanation that made sense to Von. He guessed Jugg had come to Texas with Rat. Why the two men had been separated, Von would never know. But he did know that Jugg was not close enough to save Rat from his gut-wrenching murder. Von suspected that after Jugg lost contact with Rat, the behemoth made his way to the hotel where Rat had first made his appearance. That meant Jugg was waiting when Von returned to clear out his room and grab the diamonds. That also meant that Jugg had followed him to his second property and had been keeping an eye on the place, knowing that at some point, Von would return.

Although this was most likely how Jugg had gotten intel on the location, it was a hard pill to swallow. Von knew that he'd been vigilant when he retrieved his diamonds from the hotel. He would have sworn that no one had followed him to the vacant house where he stashed the tracker or to the house where Jugg had ambushed him. But he could think of no other way for Jugg to find the place.

In any event, he realized he was foolish for not expecting this outcome. A four-man crew had broken into the Campbell heir's home and stolen the diamonds. After dispatching Rat and Katrina, he should've known Jugg would be the next threat. This was poetic justice. He could almost hear Saul giving the team their marching orders.

What he did, he took from you. All of you. If you want what's rightfully yours, you have to go and get it. Rat gave you a head start. The tracker will tell you exactly where he's hiding. The rest is up to you...

So far, all of Von's former partners in crime had been taken down in glorious fashion. Von thought Rat's death was the most gruesome, but after clawing himself from beneath Jugg's considerable girth, he realized the giant's suffering had not yet come to an end. Jugg's nose bled so profusely, Von looked as if he'd been stabbed. Lola watched him in stunned silence as he staggered to his feet. At that moment, she wasn't aware that none of the blood staining his torso belonged to him.

As Von rubbed his sore neck and struggled to get his breathing under control, they were both aware of more ragged breaths coming from the downed man. Jugg hadn't moved his arms or legs. Even when Von crawled from beneath him, the big man hadn't stirred. But there was no denying he was still alive. His chest swelled with each inhalation. His head was turned to the side. Lola saw that his eyes were wide open. Unblinking.

Finally, she found her voice. With her next words, she offered a summation of what they were witnessing. She hoped she was wrong but could think of no other explanation.

"I think he's paralyzed."

Looking down at the body, Von nodded. His face was slick with sweat and blood. His skin tone ashen. His voice was raspy when he spoke.

"I th – I think you're right."

After losing their fight so badly, Von thought he'd feel nothing but contempt for his old colleague. But as he looked down at the mortally wounded man, he was surprised that his overriding emotion was pity. Unlike Rat and Saul, Jugg had never done anything to wrong Von. He had only come to Overbrook Meadows because Saul had convinced him that Von stole from them. That was technically true, but it wasn't the full story. Von doubted if Saul had told him that he planned to steal from Von first. In any event, he couldn't fault Jugg for the way he'd chosen to respond. Jugg was like a bull in a China shop. Brute force was all he knew.

But he also had a softer side.

As Von knelt next to the body, he thought about a conversation he and Jugg had a few months ago, long before trickery had divided the crew and pit them against each other. After receiving the spoils from a smaller score, one that netted them nearly a quarter million each, Von had asked Jugg what he did with all the money he was making. The two men had sat on one of the large sofas at Saul's luxurious estate. They didn't normally hang out after receiving their payment, but Saul had offered them a celebratory drink before they hit the road. Rat and Katrina declined. Von and Jugg took a seat and allowed their boss to serve them.

In response to Von's question, Jugg replied gruffly, "What are you doing with *your* money?" He had a rich, Floridian accent.

Von's smile was quick and disarming. "I'm saving it, most of it. When I retire, I was thinking about getting into real estate."

With a smack of his thick lips, Jugg had said, "So you wanna go from robbing the rich to stealing from the poor..."

Von chuckled at that. "How is that stealing from the poor?"

"Let me guess, you wanna buy some houses for cheap, remodel 'em, and rent 'em out to some poor saps who can't afford to buy a house outright."

Von frowned and shrugged. "Yeah, I guess so. Don't think that's stealing, though. Everybody needs a place to stay."

"That's right," Jugg said. "And if somebody's gotta make it harder for those people to be homeowners. Might as well be you, right?"

Von took a sip of his drink and told him, "I don't like where this conversation is going. I was the one who asked you first, remember?"

"I'm saving most of it for my daughters and my grandkids."

"*Grandkids?*"

Jugg didn't have any gray hairs in his beard. Von had never asked directly how old he was, but he'd always figured the strongman was in his late thirties.

"I got three of 'em," Jugg confirmed. "One of my daughters is popping pills. Fentanyl. Not sure how long before CPS steps in, but I wanna be ready to help when they do. If it comes to it, I know they won't let me take the grandkids – not with my rap sheet and no real job for the past decade. But if I can get my other daughter to step in, it'll save my grandkids from the foster system. My other daughter, I know she don't want that responsibility. But if I could make it to where she's a stay at home mom, not even worrying about the bills, I think she'd do the right thing."

Von was surprised by Jugg's compassion and insight. Compared to his own selfish ambitions, Jugg was virtually a saint.

With their only true heart-to-heart in mind, Von hoped the large man felt no pain as he used his thumb and forefinger to pinch Jugg's damaged nose closed. With the same hand, he held his palm over Jugg's mouth.

Jugg's body did not react to what was happening to him. His severed spine prevented him from mounting even the slightest defense. But his eyes, they fought with everything he had in him. His fiery blue orbs stared at Von with full understanding of what was happening to him. They were accusatory and damning. They pleaded with him. They cursed him.

Von had to look away.

He looked up at Lola and found the same condemnation in her eyes. She didn't speak, and maybe she didn't feel that way, but that was the way Von interpreted the way she was staring at him.

Rather than look away again, he held her gaze as Jugg's lungs fought valiantly to suck in just one more breath of air.

The breath never came.

Von maintained the pressure on his mouth and nose for a few more minutes, until his fingers began to cramp from the effort. When he finally released him, he was sure

Jugg was dead. Still, he sat back on his haunches and watched the body for another minute.

With a sigh, he rose to his feet. He did not know how he and Lola would manage to lug the dead man to the Tahoe before following through with their plan to torch the vehicle, leaving it in some dark, desolate place.

But that's exactly what they did.

∞ ∞ ∞ ∞ ∞ ∞ ∞

"Are you alright?"

Von understood that was a stupid question that he had no right to ask. Of course Lola wasn't alright. The things they'd done in the past couple of hours – the things he'd put her through – would reverberate through her psyche for the rest of her life. She would never be the same free-spirited woman she was before their paths crossed at the bank less than one week ago.

And it was all his fault.

He piloted the rental car on the dark, still densely populated highway, headed back to their hotel room. In the trunk of the Infiniti was fifteen million dollars' worth of diamonds. He had changed clothes after hauling Jugg's body to the backseat of the Tahoe, but he hadn't bathed. He felt as filthy as he did when he dropped off another body at a duck pond on Saturday afternoon.

In response to his question, Lola told him, "Yeah. I'm okay."

She stared straight ahead, not really watching the traffic or the highway. She'd been in this position for so long, Von worried that she was slipping into a catatonic stupor. Hearing her speak did not alleviate these fears.

"I'm sorry," he told her. "I know you're not okay. How could you be?"

"You don't have to keep apologizing."

She looked his way then. Stress and fatigue made her eyelids appear heavy. Her lack of emotion was troubling. Von didn't want to see her cry, but seeing her void of emotion was just as bad.

"I didn't have to go with you," she reminded him. "You tried to leave me behind. I told you I wanted to go."

"But you had no idea what you were getting yourself into."

Her eyes back on the road, she told him, "I knew it would be dangerous. You told me."

"But even I didn't know what was gonna happen. At least if you tell me why you wanted to come, if I could understand, maybe it'll make me feel better about this..."

The moment the words left his lips, Von realized how selfish that sounded. He had traumatized this woman, yet *he* wanted *her* to make him feel better. He felt like he was going crazy. When he was in this alone, everything was simpler. If he made the wrong decisions, he would face the consequences alone. Lola was essentially his dependent. Von didn't understand how to navigate this new responsibility.

Looking his way again, she asked, "What difference does it make why I wanted to come? It's over now. What happened happened."

"It matters," he told her. "I can't explain why, but it does."

She sighed. When she didn't begin to speak right away, he thought she wasn't going to answer. But then she said, "A few reasons."

Von shot glances at her. It was dark, and he was traveling at the posted 75 miles per hour. His attention was evenly divided between her eyes and the road.

"I didn't want to be left alone," she said. "When you were gone earlier today, I damn near went crazy waiting for you to come back. I didn't want to go through that again."

Von understood that, but he didn't think it was a good enough reason for her to get caught up in a murder. She continued speaking.

She said, "I told you we were in this together. I know that sounds stupid, because it's stupid to me too. Every time I say it, I understand that it doesn't make any sense. But that's the way I feel. We went on our first date two days ago. That's not enough time to figure out how you feel about somebody, but this is different. I feel like I've known you for a lot longer. I got feelings for you. If you would've asked me this morning if those feelings were so strong I'd be willing to kill for you, I would've said hell no. But when I was put in a position to do something like that, I did what I had to do."

Von believed that she meant what she said, but at the same time, he remained skeptical. Did she really do that for him – or was self-preservation the overriding factor that caused her to intervene? If Jugg had killed him, and she was still standing there, he would've turned his vengeance on her. Then again, when she saw what was happening in the hallway, she could've turned tail and bolted from the house, if she was only interested in saving herself.

He couldn't deny that he had feelings for her as well. Although he would've done the same for her, he'd never been with a woman who was willing to risk everything she had to make sure he was okay. Rather than elation, her proclamation made him feel worse about their predicament.

What they had done should bond them for life. But how lofty was that ambition?

He became quiet, deep in thought, for the rest of the ride to the hotel.

Lola was content with the silence. She didn't speak either.

∞ ∞ ∞ ∞ ∞ ∞ ∞

Von felt as if a huge weight was lifted from him when they entered their hotel room. This place, as small as it was, felt like their home. He felt safe there. He was glad that he wasn't there alone.

He knew Lola wanted to bathe, but she insisted that he go first. Although he'd changed his shirt and pants, there was dried blood on his neck, plenty more beneath his shirt. Thankfully, none of this blood was his. Von was all for chivalry, but Lola had a point. If he sat down while waiting for her to shower, he'd spread more of Jugg's DNA throughout the hotel.

"Okay," he told her. "I won't be long."

He left the bathroom ten minutes later feeling refreshed yet exhausted. Lola was waiting, sitting on his bed. She stepped into the bathroom with a bundle of clothes in hand. Von took the seat she'd vacated on the bed and busied himself with his cellphone for a few minutes. And then it struck him that although he'd brought the cases that contained the diamonds, he didn't check them before leaving the house where Jugg made his last stand. It was doubtful that Jugg had found them; he wouldn't have stuck around if he got what he'd come for. But Von wouldn't be able to sleep until he knew for sure.

He stood and crossed the room to retrieve the cases from the top of his nightstand. He placed them on the bed and checked them both. Everything was exactly as he'd left it. He was still admiring the diamonds when Lola emerged from the bathroom behind him. She started to walk past, but curiosity made her pause and look over his shoulder. The sight of the diamonds stopped her in her tracks. She stepped closer, watching, saying nothing.

Before closing the cases, Von looked back at her. She was wearing a slip dress he'd bought at the mall earlier that day. It wasn't overtly sexy, but it didn't take much to deepen her allure.

He asked her, "Do you want to see them, up close?"

She frowned slightly and then looked down at her hands, which were filled with the dark clothes she'd worn that night.

"Put those in that bag," he said, gesturing towards the shopping bag where he'd deposited the clothes he had on that night.

Her sleepwear creeped precariously up her thighs as she bent to place the clothes in the bag. Von wondered if she was wearing panties under the slip. He forced the thought from his mind.

She returned to him, just as he removed one of the boxes from the case. Inside, a single diamond glistened like a samurai's knife. Lola didn't want to touch anything so valuable, but the diamond was safely enclosed in the box. She could see it clearly through the glass lid. She took the box from him. As she studied the precious stone, an electric charge rolled down her frame and made her legs weaken. Worried that she might actually fall, she took a seat on the bed. She returned the box to him.

If Von noticed her physical reaction, he was kind enough to not mention it. He returned the box to its place in the case and closed both of them. He returned them to the nightstand and then climbed onto the bed. Lola did not question whether it was okay to stretch out next to him. She simply did so – much to the delight of Von, who did not want to sleep alone tonight.

Before rolling towards her, he turned off the light on the nightstand. The bathroom light was still on, but the door was partially closed. The illumination from that area served as a nightlight, rather than an irritation.

Lola pulled the sheets up to her shoulders and rolled towards him. In the darkness, they faced each other. Von reached and placed a hand on her side. He inched forward and kissed her softly on the lips. She returned the affection before rolling away from him. He wasn't sure what to make of this until she backed closer in his direction. When she was settled, her back rested against his chest, and her bottom pressed against his crotch. He sighed gratefully and draped an arm around her.

They spooned, quietly and contentedly before she spoke again.

"What are you gonna do next? Are you ready to sell the diamonds?"

Speaking with his lips close to the back of her head, he told her, "I think I could try. Everyone in my crew is dead. I doubt if anyone else will come looking for me. But the only way to know for sure is to cut off the head of the snake."

After a couple of beats, she said, "You mean Saul?"

"Yeah."

"You feel like you need to talk to him or..."

"I think we're past the point of talking. None of the people he sent for me wanted to talk."

"Does that mean you're going to California?"

"Yeah, I have to. I gotta take the fight directly to him. I gotta finish it."

Lola's blood chilled. "You told me he's well protected."

"He is. And that's the reason I have to go. He has the means to send another crew after me. And another after that, if they don't get what they want. It'll never end until either he or I is dead. It would be stupid for me to wait around for him, knowing Rat or one of the others probably told him where I am. I'm sure they gave him the addresses to both my houses – and yours too."

She rolled toward him. Face-to-face in the darkness, he could barely make out her expression. The only light source illuminated from the bathroom, which she had her back to.

"So, this is about me?" she said. "You feel like you have to go after him to protect me?"

"It's always been about you, ever since Rat showed up at your house. I want to keep the diamonds, but they don't matter, if I can't keep you safe. If all of this was for me, I could've skipped town, left the country, and lived happily ever after."

"Why can't we still do that?" she wondered. "That would be easier than going after someone who has you outnumbered, outgunned."

"I don't think you know what you're saying."

Lola felt like she did, but she didn't respond.

"You have family here," he said.

"So do you."

"Yes, but I've been living detached from them for a long time. I'm sure you see your peeps every week, maybe more than that."

Lola didn't respond to that either. Von was right. Her mother would go crazy if she decided to up and leave, and never return to Overbrook Meadows.

"Then I should go with you," she stated.

He shook his head. "Every time we've tried that, you ended up deeper in a mess that you don't have anything to do with. We killed a man tonight. I know you haven't really processed what happened, but taking a life is one of the worst things you'll ever do. It's not easy to bounce back from that and go back to living a normal life."

"If I hadn't been there tonight, you would've died," she said. "You think you've got everything under control, but you needed me. If it's just you against Saul and all his men in California, you'll need me there too."

"You telling me you're willing to kill again? For me? You need to make that make sense, because I know that's not who you are. I remember how you reacted to what happened to Rat a couple of days ago. Even after he tied you up, with full intention of killing you, you didn't want me to hurt him. I don't understand how you changed so much since then."

"I don't either," she said honestly. "When that happened, I really thought that if we let him go, it would all go away. But now I know better. Now I'm willing to do whatever it takes to make our threats leave us alone for good."

"You don't have to go with me, though. I'm sure I can take care of it."

"And what if you don't? What if you get in trouble, and no one's there to watch your back? If they get you, what do you think they'll do to me?"

"I'm leaving the diamonds with you," he said. "If I don't return, you can sell them, buy you a new house in a different part of town. A different city, if you want to. They'll never find you. I'll let you know how to get some of the money to my folks, but the rest would be yours."

"First of all, I don't know how to sell those diamonds. All I know is to take one to the pawn shop, and I'll probably get arrested once they find out where they're from. Second, if they know where I live, it wouldn't take much to get my name. I'm screwed either way. But at least if I'm with you, then I have some control over my destiny."

With a sigh he said, "I can't make this decision right now."

"You don't have to. When do you plan to leave?"

"I wanted to head out tomorrow, but I have to take care of my houses first. They both look like crime scenes. I know some folks who'll come and take care of 'em, make it look like nothing ever happened. They're discreet, really good at what they do."

"So, you're leaving the day after tomorrow?"

He nodded. "Yeah. I think so."

"Good." She kissed him again before rolling away. She pressed her back against him again. "That gives me a day to make you see things my way."

Von frowned in the darkness, but he draped his arm over her, loving her close up scent and warmth. He didn't think Lola was foolish, but he could not accept that she was willing to die for this – for him. If her decisions were made for self-preservation, he could understand that. But if that was her only motivation, having possession of the diamonds could solve that problem. Money can't buy you love, but it can certainly buy you safety.

Was it love?

Von pushed the thought from his mind as quickly as it had entered. He was afraid to admit that the L word had been in his thoughts. He refused to entertain the possibility that Lola's feelings for him might be sliding towards the same uncharted territory.

He closed his eyes, but sleep was elusive.

In the quietness of the hotel, he heard Jugg struggling to suck breaths through his pinched nostrils.

After five restless minutes, he was grateful when Lola rolled his way again and said, "I can't sleep. You wanna talk about something – something other than diamonds and murder and why you think I shouldn't go to California with you, when it's obvious that I should."

Smiling, he said, "Sure. What you got in mind?"

"Tell me about when you were in high school," she offered. "I know you were a nerd. What was that like for you?"

He chuckled. "I never said I was a nerd."

"You have a degree in computer science. That's not the kind of thing you discover an interest in later in life. When you were in high school, you had to be pretty good at math or computers – or both."

"I was," he conceded. "And a lot of my classmates did think I was a nerd."

He told her about his biggest nemesis his freshman and sophomore year. Shawn Brockton knocked books out of his hands and tried to goad him into a fight every time they crossed paths, until the day Von dropped his books on his own and knocked the shit out of him in the middle of the cafeteria. After that, Shawn and all of the other bullies at North Side High School left him alone.

In return, Lola told him about a girl named Latisha who hated her guts in high school, presumably because Lola was fair-skinned and skinny, and Latisha was neither of these things. Lola never fought Latisha, but she bested her by winning Prom Queen their senior year. Midway through her story, Lola began to doze off. When she stopped speaking, Von realized she'd fallen asleep.

He lie there and watched her for a few minutes, admiring her innocence and tenacity, before he too was off to dreamland.

CHAPTER THIRTEEN
THE FINAL CHAPTER
LOOSE ENDS

Three days later, under the cover of night, Von sat in a black on black Charger on the outskirts of the gated complex where Saul felt safe enough to rest his head. This was his second day in California. On the first night, Von came to this same location to conduct the surveillance that was typical for a residence he planned to infiltrate. But tonight's affair was far from typical. Not only was the home occupied, but it was well protected. Von knew of at least three armed security personnel on the premises.

He had already hacked into the mansion's security system using his laptop and decade's worth of knowhow. Before exiting his vehicle, he studied all forty of the home's security cameras before transferring control of the system to his cellphone. He stepped out into the darkness with a pistol holstered on his hip. He reached into the backseat of the Charger and grabbed a long gun. He used the attached strap to secure it on his back. He quietly closed the car door and sucked in a cool breath of air as he turned and began the final march onto his nemesis' property.

The nighttime air was brisk. The wooded area surrounding the mansion was no doubt home to local wildlife, but Von heard no sounds, other than his own soft footsteps. The wrought iron fence that encircled the property was as ineffective as it was antiquated. It would prevent deer from encroaching onto the homestead, but scaling it posed no challenge for Von, despite the ornamental spikes at the top of the enclosure. Of course, the fence was only the first line of defense for Saul's sprawling complex. The kingpin was mostly reliant on his security system, which Von now had total control over. The guards posed a different challenge, but Von was confident he could bypass them just as easily.

He spotted the first obstacle a moment after he landed on the other side of the fence. Saul's yard was vast, the grass cut low, with dozens of trees that provided excellent cover as he crept closer to the home, which was nearly 100 yards away. With the scope on his rifle, he didn't have to get very close before taking a knee beneath the canopy of a large oak tree. He removed the rifle from his back and took aim at the guard who was standing on a side porch. Von brought the gun into firing position, bracing the stock in the crook of his shoulder. As he stared through the scope, he would've sworn the man was looking directly at him. Von held his position, not daring to move an inch. A moment later, the man looked away, and Von realized he hadn't seen him.

He lowered the weapon and chambered a round. Despite the time he'd invested in the stealth of this mission, there was no way to avoid the metallic sound of this small action. Von brought the rifle into firing position again. He stared through the scope and saw that the guard was looking his way again. Was that really a person the guard saw in the darkness, crouched next to the tree. Or was Von merely a bush that was playing tricks on his eyes? If the guard had more time to consider this, it would have occurred to him that all of the bushes on the property were adjacent to the house. There were no free standing bushes in the depths of the yard.

But the guard did not have time to make this connection.

Von pulled the trigger. The silencer on the barrel muted most but not all of the explosive echo of the rifle. Von was sure the shot would not be heard inside the house, but he suspected at least one of the guards on the perimeter might be alerted. If the gunshot wasn't enough to draw their attention, the sound of the first guard going down would surely do it.

If Von was the malicious killer Lola initially thought him to be, the guard's face, neck or chest would've exploded in a bright spray of blood. But the rounds he'd loaded into the rifle had been converted to carry specialized tranquilizers. The chemicals were similar to the dart he'd used on Katrina. But rather than a dart, the bullet portion of the rounds were replaced with plastic capsules that carried the potent drugs.

The capsule struck the guard with less velocity and power, compared to a bullet, but the effect was virtually the same. The man immediately went down. Even from a distance, Von heard him moaning as the drugs streamed through his blood. He wasn't surprised when guard number 2 rounded the corner to see what the problem was. Von chambered another round and watched the second guard through his scope. The man drew his weapon, a menacing assault rifle, as he approached his fallen brethren. Von waited until he knelt next to the first guard before he fired a second time. This shot was true as well.

The second guard did not fall immediately.

Instead, he gripped his abdomen, his head turning in the direction of the bush that most certainly was not a standalone bush next to the oak tree. Von considered pulling the trigger a third time, but through his scope, he saw that the man's face had gone slack. His eyes began to droop at the same pace as his body. A moment later, he gingerly sat on his ass, next to the first guard, and then decided that lying down was more comfortable.

Von did not have to check his watch to start the timer on how long the two men would remain incapacitated. He knew they would be asleep for a minimum of four hours. He planned to be long gone by then.

He held the gun with both hands as he left his cover and began to encircle the west side of the property. He remained on the outskirts of the yard, using the trees to cloak his approach. He spotted the third guard posted near the back door of the main house. This man also toted an assault rifle. He was ready for anything. He'd most likely been warned that Von had taken out his former crew and might pay them a visit sometime soon. But he hadn't heard the commotion on the other side of the house, and he didn't see his target lurking in the darkness, now no more than thirty yards away. Von fired again. The guard never knew what hit him.

Von waited a few minutes, until he was sure the tranquilizers had taken effect, before he removed his phone from his pocket and checked all of Saul's cameras again. He knew there were no other guards outside of the home before the cameras confirmed this. He returned the rifle to the strap around his back and drew his pistol. The magazine in this weapon contained live rounds. If he was surprised by another guard, Von would be forced to take his life. But unless the fourth guard was hiding out of view of *all* of the cameras, Von was confident this night would not include the blood of an innocent bystander. The cameras had revealed the location of the last man standing at this residence. And Saul was by no means innocent.

Von casually approached the back of the home. He looked down at the third guard and found him snoring peacefully, his rifle still within reach of his useless hands. On the hip opposite his holster, Von toted a tool belt that contained all of the gadgets necessary to bypass the lock on the patio door. A minute later, he stepped inside of the mansion. He didn't bother closing the door behind him. The alarm system alert that this entrance had been left open came to his phone now, rather than Saul's.

Standing in a darkened kitchen that was large enough to serve a restaurant, Von checked the cameras one last time. Nothing had changed. He did not bother to check the rooms to his right or left as he marched slowly towards the main living room. At one a.m., most of the lights inside the home were off. He headed for the only source of illumination at the end of the large hallway. He readied his weapon before stepping into the large, brightly lit space, but there was no need.

Saul sat alone on a leather loveseat. He was awake and unarmed. As his head turned in Von's direction, his eyes registered acceptance, rather than surprise. Von did not lower his weapon. Not only had Saul proven himself to be wily, but this was his home turf. Von would not have been surprised if Saul had a pistol or two tucked away in the chair.

"Hello, Von," the older man said.

Von nodded slightly. "Hey, Saul."

Saul was Caucasian of Jewish descent. In his late fifties, the top of his head was mostly bald. Rather than go for the full Kojak, he retained the salt and peppery hair on the sides and back of his head. Saul was fit – not just for his age. His hobbies included cycling, hunting and mountain climbing. He wore a designer tee with cargo shorts. On the coffee table next to him, a drinking glass contained two fingers of dark liquor.

Von stepped closer, so he could keep an eye on Saul's hands. The room's décor was immaculate. Even the gaudy paintings on the walls matched the furnishing. Von approached Saul on his right side and checked the large TV mounted on the wall to see what had held Saul's attention before he entered the room. He wasn't surprised to see a grid view of the security cameras. In the videos Saul was watching, Von saw the security guards moving about the perimeter of the home. They appeared fully alert and competent.

"How'd you get past them?" Saul asked, following his gaze.

Von met his blue eyes. "You knew I was coming? Is that why you had them out there?"

"I had a hunch," Saul agreed.

"If you thought I was coming, you should've known better than to rely on your security system. Not saying yours isn't topnotch, but it's not better than the one at the Campbell's mansion."

"My system has been compromised?"

Von nodded. "The feed you've been watching is on a loop. Your guards are alive, sleeping peacefully. They'll be back to their old selves in about four hours."

"Really?" Saul's eyes narrowed. "How'd you manage that?"

"A new concoction I've been working on. Tested it for the first time tonight. To be honest, I'm surprised it worked so well."

Saul brought a hand up.

Von was ready to pull the trigger, but the older man simply rubbed his clean-shaven chin. "Impressive." He sighed. "Well, you haven't killed me, so I'm guessing there's something you want from me..."

"There is. I wanna know why you betrayed me and then sent my crew to take me out."

"You're the one who took off with the diamonds. Most would argue that it was you who betrayed us."

"Don't try to manipulate me, like you did with Rat. I told you I wanted to retire after the last job. All I wanted was my share of the fifteen mil'. It could've been so simple."

"And yet, after I agreed to your terms, you decided to split with all of the diamonds. You don't think your crew had a right to come after you to get back what was rightfully theirs?"

"And you don't think Rat told me about your plan to double-cross me?"

Saul tried not to react to that news, but his eyes betrayed him, if only for a moment.

"Rat told me about your little powwow with him before we did the job," Von informed him. "You planned to swap the real diamonds with fake ones and send me on my way with a bunch of worthless trinkets. I don't know why you thought you could trust Rat with that plan. He's as two-faced as the day is long."

"If he's as unreliable as you say," Saul replied, "and I'm not doubting that he is – or *was*, then why do you believe he was telling you the truth about me? What proof do you have, other than the word of someone you just described as *two-faced*, that I planned to betray you?"

Von accepted that Saul had a point, but he also understood that this man was supremely cunning. Plus, everyone knows that a man will say anything when he's staring down the barrel of a pistol.

"So," Von said, "your assertion is that Rat was lying, you never planned to betray me, and as far as the crew was concerned, I was the one who had betrayed all of you?"

"That's certainly the way it looks," Saul said. "But after hearing this about Rat, I understand why you did what you did. I wish we could've had this conversation before any blood was shed. I take it they're all dead, Katrina and Jugg too?"

Von nodded.

"You're far more resourceful than I gave you credit for," Saul said. "Any chance we can let bygones be bygones. I could really use a man like you on my side. We could put another team together, with you in charge of them. After a couple of years, we'll make so much money, the diamonds you took will seem like pocket change."

Von didn't consider that before shaking his head. "No. I told you I want to retire. That hasn't changed."

"Understood. So, why did you come back? You have the diamonds, and you've vanquished your foes. Why not take the diamonds and enjoy your retirement?"

"I came back because I wanted to know if it was really over – or if you plan to send more men after me."

"I don't believe that," Saul said. "You obviously don't trust me. Why would you come this far and go through all this trouble just to have me lie to your face? But, for the record, no I do not plan to send more people after you. If you managed to take out Jugg, there's no one on my payroll who'd be able to track you down and bring the diamonds back to me. It's not worth it to invest any more resources into this mess."

"Not even for fifteen million?"

"I know that's a lot of money – *for you*," Saul said. "And you know that's not a lot of money for me. I'm okay with you keeping the diamonds and selling them and never crossing my path again. I'm sure you're okay with that scenario as well."

"I am," Von agreed. "And if that's truly how you feel, then I'm sure you wouldn't mind giving me the contact info for a buyer."

"Really?" Saul grinned at that. "Are you telling me you've got everything you ever wanted, but you can't find a way to sell it?"

"I haven't tried," Von said honestly. "I'm sure I could figure it out, but I don't wanna stress myself trying to find someone I can trust. I know that you usually have a buyer lined up before we do a job."

"You're right," Saul said. "It took years for me to build my reputation and come in contact with the right people. You never know who's working for the feds these days. I do have a buyer for the diamonds, but he'll never trust you. He was expecting to meet with me directly."

"He'll trust me if you call him and tell him to trust me."

"Fine," Saul said. "I'll call him first thing tomorrow morning."

Von shook his head. "I'll be gone by then – unless you want me to stick around. We can hang out, have a slumber party, I suppose."

With a grunt, Saul told him, "No, I do not want that at all. How about if I give you his number and give you my word that I will call him tomorrow?"

"How about you give me his number and call him now? If you want me to leave, that's the only way it'll work."

"Von, it is one o'clock in the morning. Depending on which coast my friend is on, it may be even later for him. You may not understand the importance of maintaining the professional relationships I've cultivated, but surely you can be respectful of my buyer's time. If I call him at this hour, he will know that I made the call under duress."

Von's eyes narrowed as he considered this. "Okay," he conceded. "Give me his number and give me your word that you will call him in the morning."

"I give you my word."

With his free hand, Von reached and rubbed his forehead. "Saul, I need you to understand that if I leave here with the number and something falls through tomorrow, I'll be back. I'll kill your guards, and I'll kill you. But it won't be quick and easy – not for you. I'll make sure you regret trying to double-cross me the first and second time."

"I already told you I didn't double-cross you the first time, and I'm not about to do it now."

"Whatever," Von said. "Just give me the number."

"Okay, but I have to get up for that."

"It's not in your cellphone?" Von asked, nodding towards the cellular on the coffee table next to his drinking glass.

With a muted chuckle, Saul said, "I would never save the number of a contact such as this in my cellphone. I have it in my safe, in a bible, coded, spread out on multiple pages."

That explanation sounded too convoluted to be a lie. It also matched the cunning Von knew Saul was capable of.

"Okay," he said. "Go get it. Get up slowly. Keep your hands in view the whole time."

Saul cracked a smile. "Yes, sir." He placed his palms flat on the chair's armrest to brace himself as he rose to his feet.

Von took a step back in preparation for a surprise lunge attack, but Saul didn't try anything foolish. He walked away from the loveseat, and Von followed him through the mostly dark home.

"Wait, slow down," Von said when Saul turned and headed down one of the hallways. He rounded the same corner and found Saul standing still, waiting obediently.

"Can I go now?"

"Yeah," Von said, his gun aimed at the center of the man's back. "Go ahead."

Midway down the hallway, Saul turned towards one of the doors. He pushed it open and stepped inside, pausing long enough to flip the light switch. Von followed him and found himself standing in a bedroom that was nearly twice the size of the last hotel room he and Lola shared in Overbrook Meadows. This room was as opulent as the rest of the mansion, but Von did not spare the time to admire the furnishings. Saul was on the move again, heading towards an open closet.

"I have a safe in here," Saul explained.

He flipped another light switch, illuminating a walk in closet that would make the average New Yorker grit his teeth in disgust. It had been years since Von lived in a cramped apartment, but even he wanted to comment on the overall unnecessariness of it all. Saul didn't have a family that Von knew of. Why did he need so much space? How many square feet were enough to satisfy America's filthy rich?

Towards the back of the closet, a dozen suits hung in garment bags. Saul pushed garments to the side, revealing a medium size safe. He looked over his shoulder to see if Von was still watching him. He was. Saul did not ask Von to avert his attention as he entered the combination for the safe. A moment later, he pulled it open.

Von stepped closer and to the side, so he could see what was inside. In addition to a small fortune in cash, Von saw an assortment of documents, five or more small boxes that were similar to the ones in his diamond cases, and a bible. The good book was the only thing Saul retrieved from the safe. He turned towards Von as he flipped through a few of the pages. He paused, turned several more pages, paused again, repeated this process, and finally he closed the book.

"I have the number. Are you ready?"

Von frowned and asked him, "How did you get the phone number from that book?"

Saul smiled at him. "I told you; I wrote the number in my bible. I used a code, in case anyone ever tried to find it."

"Show me your code."

Still smiling, Saul said, "Do you want to see it because you don't believe me, or because you might want to use it yourself one day?"

"Both."

"Okay."

Saul opened the book to the first page he'd turned to, in the book of Genesis. He held the bible out for Von to see. "You see this date and the notes I made under it?"

Von nodded.

"The date is actually the beginning of the phone number. The notes look like the highlights from the passage I read that day. But at the end, you see how I wrote Com 1..."

Von saw that, but it didn't mean anything to him.

"My buyer is named Phillip Comstock. 'Com' let's me know whose phone number this is. The one lets me know the date is the first part of the phone number. I just had to flip a few pages until I found 'Com 2,' and the last part of the number is the date above 'Com 3.' It sounds more complicated than it actually is."

Von didn't doubt that, but he was impressed with Saul's coding system. He removed his phone from his pocket and created a new contact. "Alright. What's the number?"

Saul gave it to him.

Von saved the number and returned the phone to his pocket. "Okay. I guess that takes care of that."

"Yes. And I will be sure to call him first thing in the morning to let him know you'll be in contact with him."

Von nodded. "I suppose that's it then. Once this is done, you won't hear from me again – unless you do something stupid, like tell Mr. Comstock to set me up, so you can get the diamonds back."

"You need not worry about that," Saul said, smiling. "My buyers are white collar all the way. They wouldn't meddle in anything dangerous. Mr. Comstock doesn't even bring a weapon when I meet with him. I'm sure he'll be a little miffed about meeting with you rather than me, but at the end of the day, money is money. He won't turn away your business, as long as I tell him he can trust you."

Von didn't like the idea of putting so much faith in the word of this man, but he didn't see a way around it. If things didn't work out with this Comstock person, he was sure he could find a way to sell the diamonds on his own. It might take a little longer, but in the end, he'd have his money, and he could officially retire from his life of crime.

"Okay," he said. "I'm out then." Rather than turn his back on Saul and whatever else might be hidden in the closet, he told him, "You go first."

"A skeptic till the very end," Saul noticed. But he didn't protest. He walked out of the closet with Von right behind him.

Back in the living room, Von considered whether he should back all the way out of the house, with his gun trained on Saul the whole time, and continue backing his way through the back yard, all the way to the spot where he'd jumped the fence. He decided against it. At some point he'd have to turn his back on his former boss. If Saul had something up his sleeve, he'd eventually have a chance to show his hand, no matter how Von played it.

Though betrayal was on the forefront of his mind as he turned and headed towards the kitchen, where the patio doors remained open, Von did not expect Saul to betray him so quickly. Von had taken no more than a few steps before he heard the unmistakable sound of a bullet being chambered in a weapon behind him. He stopped in his tracks and raised both hands without being prompted.

Behind him, Saul said, "Bend over, slowly, and put your gun on the floor. Don't try anything foolish."

Von did as he was told. When he rose to a standing position, now unarmed, he asked, "Can I turn around now?"

Saul told him, "Sure, Von."

Von turned and saw that Saul was now armed with a small but no less lethal handgun. He had dropped his bible. Von looked down and saw that it was open on the floor. The middle pages had been hollowed out.

"The old pistol in the bible trick," he surmised.

"Old, but you still fell for it," Saul said.

Von shook his head in disappointment. "Yeah, I guess I did. So, what now? If you wanted me dead, you could've shot me in the back."

"I do want you dead," Saul told him. "But I want my diamonds more. What happens now is I call some guys over, and they take you back to Texas. You give up the diamonds, and *maybe* I'll tell them to let you live."

"That's not a bad plan," Von said. "But before we do that, don't you want me to fix your security system, so you can see what's really going on with your cameras?"

Saul frowned. "I don't think that matters right now."

"Oh, I think it matters a lot," Von said. "Humor me."

Saul chuckled, shaking his head slightly. "Okay. Go for it."

"I gotta dig in my pocket for my phone," Von said. "I promise, there's nothing in here but an iPhone." He reached into his front pocket.

Saul watched him closely, saying nothing.

Von removed his phone, accessed the mansion's security system, and returned the cameras to the live feed.

Saul was standing close enough to see the television he'd been watching when Von first arrived. He glanced at the camara grid and saw that his guards were not in fact on patrol. They were all slumped and motionless. More importantly, the camera in the living room revealed a sight that made Saul's eyes widen. Before he could turn to see if his eyes were deceiving him, Von's accomplice, who'd been waiting in the wings the whole time, spoke up.

"Drop the gun," Lola said. "You should've left well enough alone."

Despite the tension in the room, Von couldn't help but laugh. "Why you gotta be so greedy?" he asked. "This is twice that you could've let me have what's legitimately mine."

Saul had recovered enough from his initial shock to maintain an even voice when he replied. "What if I kill him anyway?" he asked Lola without looking her way.

"That's cool," she said. "I know where the diamonds are. If me and Von leave together, we'll split the money. If I go back alone, it's all mine. Either way, you'll be dead the moment you pull the trigger."

Von could see Saul's brain race as he weighed his options. It didn't take him long to make the obvious decision. "Okay. I'm gonna put my gun down. Don't shoot."

The moment he placed his piece on the floor, Von bent and retrieved his. Lola came and stood at Von's side. They both watched the defeated man. Both had a handgun pointed at him.

"I know what you're thinking," Von told Lola. "After all he's been through, he'll let us walk out of here, and he won't cause us any more trouble."

"It's true," Saul said. It took a while, but he'd finally lost his cool. Sweat beaded on his mostly bald head. Even with his hands by his sides, they could see that his fingers were trembling.

"No, that wasn't what I was thinking," Lola said. She was dressed in all black, just like Von.

"What were you thinking?" he asked, more for Saul's benefit than his.

"I was thinking about what happened with Rat. You told me he'd be back if we didn't kill him, but I didn't listen."

"*No, please,*" Saul begged. "*I swear I won't come after you! Please don't do this!*"

Von thought Lola fired first.

She thought it was him.

Either way, the result was the same. Saul fell to the floor, twitching and gurgling on his own blood. The sound of the gunfire echoed through the spacious room, which was now tainted by the acrid smell of blood and gun smoke from both of their weapons.

As they trekked through the backyard, towards the Charger parked on the outskirts of the property, Lola said, "Tell me; are you glad you didn't leave me behind in Texas?"

"I am, but the way you ask that question makes me feel like you don't think I could've handled this on my own."

"I'm not saying that. Guess I wanna hear that you like having me around."

"No doubt." He looked over at her, enthralled by the way the moonlight accentuated her soft features. "Wouldn't have it any other way."

EPILOGUE

What forces are these that make me see diamonds
Whenever I close my eyes?
Princess cuts, sparkling with radiance
As brilliant as the starlit skies
It captivates my body and controls my senses
Whenever my thoughts are of you
Like the Marquise cut, it's beautifully complex
Like radiation changing its hue
It wraps my body like sweet perfumes
When I hold you in my arms
It captivates like trilliant cut necklaces
It soothes like the break of dawn
I offer you a love so deep and so pure
Lovemaking so raw and so wet
You offer me a kiss from your sweet lips
And I see cushion cuts, Asscher, baguette

Saul was both right and wrong about Phillip Comstock. While it was true the buyer did not appear armed the first time he and Von met, Comstock brought along two associates who were definitely packing heat. The men stood stoically, both dressed in athletic wear, at an upscale coffee shop in San Bernadino. The waitress who served Von and

Comstock did not offer the bodyguards a seat or inquire about why they remained standing during the breakfast.

While they ate, Von was focused on the man with the money, but he was distracted by the way the waitress walked around the two goons without acknowledging their presence. This was the first of a few oddities he encountered while selling the diamonds. During the meeting, most of the questions Comstock had were about Von, but he also inquired about Saul. He mentioned that Saul was a good friend and wondered if he would hear from him soon.

After Saul's grisly death, Von kept his ear to the news, wondering how the shady mogul's murder would be portrayed. After a few days with no word, he deduced that Saul's people had taken care of the body without reporting the incident to the police. This scenario was in line with the type of person Von knew Saul to be; he would rather go missing and never found, like Jimmy Hoffa, than allow his associates to know that someone had managed to murder him, despite the many precautions he'd taken to protect himself.

"I don't know," Von told Comstock. "I haven't heard from him in over a week. I thought he'd reach out by now."

The buyer nodded. "Yes, so did I. I was surprised that he'd give you my contact information. But if he was willing to do so, I know that he must trust you."

"I've worked with Saul for years," Von confirmed. "Most of the transactions you've had with him were due to my work. I told him I wanted to venture out on my own, and he supported my decision."

Still nodding, Comstock said, "I see. Did you bring what I asked for?"

"Yes, I have it in the car."

Initially Von was wary of leaving one of the Campbell's diamonds for the buyer to take with him and authenticate. But he understood that he had to trust Comstock as much as Comstock was willing to trust him. The diamond he brought to this meeting was still in the original box it was encased in when they pulled off the heist. The two cases in Von's possession contained 24 identical boxes in each. If the buyer took off with the one diamond, and Von never heard from him again, he still had 47 diamonds to sell. But after meeting with Comstock, he did not believe their business would end in such a manner.

"Great," the buyer said. "When we're done eating, you'll leave before me. Bruno will follow you out. You can leave it with him."

"Not a problem."

"Splendid. You should try the bacon while it's still warm," he said, gesturing towards Von's plate. "I can't have any myself, but I have fond memories of how well they prepare it here."

Von picked up a slice of caramelized bacon and devoured half of it. "You're right. It's excellent."

Comstock grinned at him. "Yes, the chefs here are outstanding."

∞ ∞ ∞ ∞ ∞ ∞ ∞

Comstock did not attend the second phase of the diamond purchase. He directed Von to a prominent bank, where the manager was waiting on him. Von was glad that he'd worn slacks with a sport coat to the meeting. Everyone in the building was dressed professionally. The manager assisted him in setting up a cash management account. Even though Von did not bring any money to deposit, he was treated as if he already had millions of dollars at this bank.

Towards the end of the meeting, the manager told him, "I understand you're expecting to sell one of your properties soon."

This was news to Von, but he nodded and said, "Yes. The deal should go through within the next week or so."

"Great," the manager said. "We appreciate your business and look forward to servicing your new account."

∞ ∞ ∞ ∞ ∞ ∞ ∞

In the third and most tense phase of the diamond purchase, Comstock, once again, was not in attendance. Von took the remaining diamonds to a high-end jeweler at 8 a.m., two hours before the business opened for the day. Inside the establishment, the middle aged owner invited Von to a back room that sufficiently shielded them from the glass storefront. After examining every diamond in both cases, a process that took nearly an hour, the man made a call and confirmed everything was as it should be.

A few moments later, Von received a call. He accepted it and heard Comstock's voice on the other end of the line.

"Von, I've made arrangements to gift you a property in Long Beach. An attorney is prepared to meet with you at 10:30 to sign the paperwork. At noon, you have an appointment with a realtor to sell the property to one of my investors. The price will be fourteen point six million. Do you find that number acceptable?"

Von was too taken aback by everything else that was said to squabble over a few hundred thousand dollars. "Yes," he told him. "I'm okay with that."

"Splendid. Do you have a pen?"

"One second."

Von retrieved a pad and pen from the jeweler, and Comstock gave him the contact information for both appointments.

Before leaving the jewelry store, it occurred to Von that he was leaving behind everything he'd murdered and risked his life for. If Comstock decided to burn him now, he would have no recourse. He had no way of contacting the buyer other than a phone number, which Comstock could simply stop answering.

He stepped out of the jewelry store in faith and attended both of the appointments Comstock had lined up for him.

Hours later, at 3:35 p.m., Von received a notification from his new bank that the money had been wired to his account. He could barely contain his elation as he transferred half of it to his other bank account, one that he'd had for over a decade. He knew the transaction would trigger an investigation, and he inwardly thanked Comstock for effectively laundering the money for him. With the documents from the attorney and the realtor, the money was legally his, above reproach.

∞ ∞ ∞ ∞ ∞ ∞ ∞

Two weeks later, Von and Lola strolled casually through Crepe Myrtle Allee at the Dallas Arboretum and Botanical Gardens. The trees lined both sides of the walkway, their limbs stretching first towards the sun and then towards each other, creating a stunning canopy that gave the appearance of walking through a large, living tunnel of beautiful flora, as if Mother Nature was stretching her hands over their love.

At the end of the path, they found a gazebo that was surrounded by stunning daffodils, hyacinths, tulips, cherry blossoms and azaleas. They sat there, talked awhile, and soon found themselves making out like teenagers. Between kisses, Lola told him that this moment, this incredible space in time, was the happiest she'd ever been. Von shared those sentiments tenfold.

They left the arboretum and climbed into Von's new ride – an Infiniti QX80. He liked the make so much when he rented one several weeks ago, that he bought one for himself. When they reached Overbrook Meadows, Von surprised Lola by taking the freeway to a seedy part of town and exiting in a neighborhood that was familiar to her, but at the time she couldn't say why. He drove in silence for a few minutes before turning onto a street that Lola had visited before. The poverty in this area was palpable. Since exiting the freeway, Lola was sure that she'd seen either a liquor store or corner store for every vacant house in the neighborhood. Her chest squeezed uncomfortably as Von piloted them closer to their destination.

Her trepidation was replaced by curiosity as they drew closer to the sight ahead. Two large moving trucks were parked on either side of the street. A bustle of activity flowed from the house on the right. Not only was it unusual for the residents of this area to hire professional movers – typically they'd find a friend with a pickup truck or rent a U-Haul if they could afford it – but it was also uncharacteristic to see so many smiles on moving day. The family saying goodbye to their dilapidated residence were not being evicted and had not been forced to leave due to a foreclosure.

As Von drove closer, Lola recognized the mother, father, and one of the older sons standing in the front yard. The head of the household was in his fifties. He gave orders to the movers and did not feel the need to carry any of the boxes himself – another oddity for moving day in the hood.

"This is Desmond Green's family," she uttered knowingly.

Von nodded.

Desmond was the child Lola had mistakenly killed on the day her brother was murdered. When she told Von about the incident, which was still the absolute worst moment of her life, she'd ask him if he could do something for Desmond's family, once the diamonds were sold. Von had told her that he would, but they hadn't spoken about it since then. Lola was surprised that he remembered. By the looks of it, he had kept his word.

Her eyes filling with tears, she asked him, "How much did you give them?"

"A million," Von said.

He'd lowered his speed as he drove between the two moving trucks. He looked through the passenger window and briefly locked eyes with Desmond's father. In that brief moment, he saw true happiness in the older man's eyes. It was the look of a man who had always believed it would take a miracle to elevate his family from their circumstances. That miracle came by way of a lawyer who contacted the Green family one week ago. According to the lawyer, an anonymous benefactor had started a trust fund after Desmond's death. Over the years, the fund had grown to one million dollars, and it could now be transferred to the bereaved family.

Von lost sight of the family as he drove between the two large trucks. A few moments later, he turned left at the next intersection and made his way back to the freeway.

Lola hadn't spoken again after asking how much Von had given the Greens. By the time they reached the freeway, she had regained her composure.

Wiping her eyes, she told him, "Thank you. You didn't have to do that for me."

Von looked her way and said, "I disagree. I know how much that meant to you. I was happy to do my part."

She smiled wistfully. She reached over and placed a hand on his thigh. He placed his hand over hers and squeezed comfortingly.

They drove in silence for a while before he looked her way again and said, "Guess where we're going now."

Lola had no idea. The day had already been filled with unexpected beauty and breathtaking spectacles. Aside from a marriage proposal, she didn't think there was anything Von could do to make her love him more.

"I don't know," she said, her heart floating in her chest. "Where are we going?"

"To the airport," he said. "I got us tickets to Florida, South Beach. Have you ever been?"

She shook her head, her eyes revealing confusion and enthusiasm. "We're going to the airport *now*? I didn't pack anything. Did you?"

"No. I figured we can pick up whatever we need when we get there."

After a bewildered chuckle, she said, "Von, I don't even have a charger for my phone. We can't just go to the airport with nothing."

"Sure we can," he said grinning. "They sell chargers at the airport. It'll actually make boarding easier, if we don't have any bags to check."

"I..." She continued smiling, shaking her head in wonderment now. "I've never done anything like that before."

"Are you saying you don't wanna go?"

"No, I'm not saying that. Of course I wanna go. I'm just not used to living like this."

"I understand. Well, do you think this is something you can learn to get used to?"

"I don't know," she gushed honestly. "I think so."

"I think so too," he said. "I think you're about to have the time of your life."

She studied his features as he smiled at her. She didn't feel worthy of this handsome, wonderful man or this new lifestyle she'd been blessed with.

Blessed?

She reflected on some of her earlier feelings about Von – how devastated she was after their first date, when she thought he'd rejected her during breakfast. That felt like ages ago, though the memory and her emotions at the time remained crystal clear.

She settled back in her seat and accepted the notion that they were headed to the airport with no luggage, and a plane would soon whisk them away to an aquatic paradise.

"When we get there," Von said, as if reading her mind, "the first thing I wanna buy you is a bikini."

"Oh," she replied. "I was hoping the *first* thing you'd want to do is chase me around the hotel room naked."

He looked her way, his dark eyes narrowed and filled with lust. "That's an even better idea," he commented. He gave the Infiniti a little more gas and merged into the left lane.

Lola's eyes slipped closed, the smile still plastered on her face.

Yes, this was definitely the kind of lifestyle she could get used to.

KEITH THOMAS WALKER

ABOUT THE AUTHOR

Keith Thomas Walker, known as the Master of Romantic Suspense and Urban Fiction, is the author of more than two dozen novels, including *Fixin' Tyrone, Life After, The Realest Ever,* the *Backslide* series, the *Brick House* series, the *Finley High* series and the *Asha and Boom* series. Keith's books transcend all genres. He has published romance, urban fiction, mystery/thriller, teen/young adult, Christian, poetry and erotica. Originally from Fort Worth, he is a graduate of Texas Wesleyan University. Keith has won numerous awards in the categories of "Best Male Author," "Best Romance," "Best Urban Fiction," "Best Young Adult Romance," "Best Duo," "Book of the Year," and "Author of the Year," from several book clubs and organizations. Visit him at www.keiththomaswalker.com.